SWISH

1996

WILLIAM THOMAS LONDON

FREE PREVIEW

When he got on campus, he notices a crowd gathering at the Quad in the middle of the campus. There was a lot of joking and laughter going on. As he approaches, he saw amongst the crowd laughing harder than anyone was Freeze.

"What's so funny?" He inquires of his friend, Freeze, as he approaches him. Freeze answers, "Dude." He spurted out between his laughter. He greets JJ with a high five. "You late dude," he says trying to control his laughter. "What?" JJ asks. "You missed out on the fun." "Look." Freeze says. Pointing towards the flagpole in the right corner of the Quad.

There hanging from the flagpole a human body. It was the pale weird looking kid. "Momma!" The weird kid yells. "Momma!" The crowd mocks him.

"Ain't that the funniest thing you ever seen." Freeze proclaims. "The funniest thing." JJ repeats half-heartedly because he was not really feeling this joke. "Momma!" The boy yells again. His underwear showed as the hook from the flagpole rope bungled his blue underwear into a wedgie. His pants were down to his ankles now and his shirt is covering his pale face. "Momma!" He yells again.

This time the rope had rotated him facing the crowd. His shirt had fallen to the ground. You could see the tears streaming down from his face. Somehow JJ did not see the humor in this prank anymore.

"Ok, Freeze that's enough." JJ says to Freeze. "Let him down."

KEYNOTE

Swish, is an inner-city adventure book that takes place in the 1990's. The story takes a serious look at adolescent bullying in High School..

To the young men I have mentored over the years:

<u>**Ecclesiastes 11:9 ESV**</u>

Rejoice, O young man, in your youth, and let your heart cheer you in the days of your youth. Walk in the ways of your heart and the sight of your eyes. But know that for all these things God will bring you into judgment.

In loving memory of:

My beloved wife, Mae Ellen (Davis) Wright

Proverbs 31:10-12 MSG

A good woman is hard to find, and worth far more than diamonds.

Mae Ellen Davis Wright

My parents:

William Leo and Amanda Ellen (Thompkins) Wright

Ephesians 6:1 NIV

Children obey your parents in the Lord, for this is right.

Rev William Leo "Willie" Wright, Sr.

Amanda Ellen Thompkins Wright

My grandparents:

Sirach 44:1 USCCB

I will now praise the godly, our ancestors, in their own time,

Jimmy Wright, Sr.

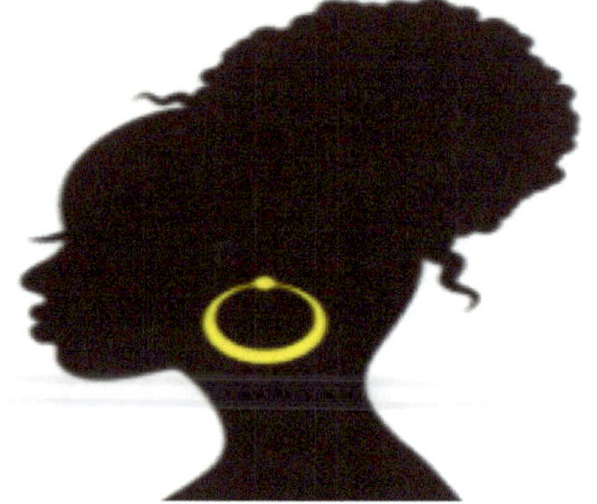

Maose "Moose" Coleman Wright

Jessie Terrell Lucas Thompkins and Claude Thompkins

Ephesians 6:1 NIV
Children obey your parents in the Lord, for this is right.

My siblings who have gone on to glory:

Marian Yvonne Wright
Lewis Rochelle Wright
Thomas (Lil Pookie) Curtis Wright
Katherine (Wright) Johnson
Deborah (Wright) Gaston
Dorothy (Dot) Jean (Wright) Dodds

Marian Yvonne Wright

Lewis Rochelle Wright

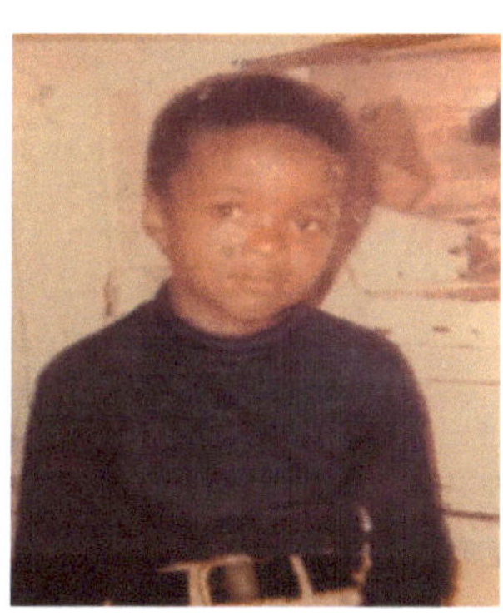

**Thomas (Lil Pookie)
Curtis Wright**

Katherine Wright Johnson

Deborah Wright Gaston

**Dorothy Jean "Dot"
Wright Dodds**

My siblings who are still on this journey with me:

Carrie E. Wright
William L. Wright, Jr.
Carl B. Wright Sr.
Willette A. (Wright) Jones
Ruth M. (Wright) Broach
Dr. Dale H. Conaway

Hebrews 13:1-2 NIV

Keep on loving one another as brothers and sisters. Do not forget to show hospitality to strangers, for by so doing some people have shown hospitality to angels without knowing it.

My Church Family

Allen Temple Missionary Baptist Church
8501 International Blvd. Oakland, Ca. 94621

Shout out to:

My Former Coworkers

Alameda County Probation Department
Oakland Unified School District (Stonehurst & Howard Elementary Schools)
Oakland Parks and Recreation

Staff and patients at:

Fresenius Kidney Care Stockton, California
where this book was written.

To the Staff of:

Weston Ranch Library Stockton, California
where some of this book was written.

Matthew 9:37
New International Version

37 Then he said to his disciples, "The harvest is plentiful but the workers are few.

SPECIAL THANKS

My niece, Jonnette Marvetta "Nettie" Jones, for lending her creative talents in creating pictures for this book.

My sister, Willette Wright Jones, for assisting, editing, arranging, and helping me complete this project.

Lonnie, you asked for my opinion so here is my two cents worth critique.

Our parents would be very proud of you and your accomplishments. Now, you know if Mama were here, I'd have to tell on you for using "cuss words" and she would have disciplined you with a sound spanking using the switch you had to go and pick off the tree in the backyard yourself.

Overall, I feel your story captures what many people like Benjamin "Swish" Swisher experience in life. Through adversity, they are able to thrive everyday even though they are being bullied and ridiculed just for being who they are. The "Swish" character was innocent and humble as well as brave enough to persevere through the challenges presented to him and was able to teach many life lessons to those who took the time to get to know him. He was also multi-talented and had a great sense of humor.

Actually, the character reminds me of you.

Willette Amanda Wright Jones

My brother in law, John R. Jones, Sr. for assistance with picture arrangements and editing.

Contents

SWISH
1995

CHAPTER 1

NEW KID ON THE BLOCK

Here he was at the podium of his graduation, June 12th, 1996. One day before his 18th birthday. Reflecting upon what had really happened that year. Preparing to give the valedictorian speech for his class. Not for himself, but for someone else. Lord knows he wasn't an academic genius. He was giving it for someone more deserving than himself. A special person that had changed the way he looked at life. He was giving the speech in his stead. Surely an honor. As he stood there waiting to speak, he reflected on how they had come to this moment. It seemed so long ago.

The year was September 1995. The beginning of his Senior year at Amanda Ellen Thompkins Senior High. The year started off like every other year. The vice principal was Ulysses Jackson, Mr. J for short. He was a big burly Black guy with a fluffy natural going bald in the middle. Only thing bushier than that Afro with the hole in the middle was that thick moustache and beard on his scraggly unshaven face. Everyone at the school knew he was the real principal. Then there was the principal, Mr. Alex Johnson. A timid, scrawny, White guy whose petite statue matched his soft-spoken voice. He was short and pale, had a clean-shaven face with thin brown hair that was graying on the edges. His skin was white as snow. Unlike Mr. Jackson, who was on a bull horn in the hallways all about campus constantly barking out marching orders, Mr. Johnson kept himself pretty much hidden in his office.

The school year started off with the same boring routine. Monday was freshman orientation day, Tuesday was school assembly, Wednesday, and Thursday were class sign up days, and Friday was teacher prep day. JJ, being a jock, with his classes already chosen for him just came to school to hangout. He had a letter in three sports, baseball, football, and basketball. He just came to school to hang out with the homies, flirt with the honeys and pick on the nerds, the dweebs. He basically hung out frolicking with the basketball team. They have had a special connection since elementary school. There was Morris Green, Big Mo, the 6'8" center who was Lanky as a giraffe but clumsy as an ox. He was the only one who had an "Afro bigger than Mr. Jackson's. (Minus the hole in the middle.) There was Dwight "Da White Boi", Rogers. Only White guy on the basketball team. (Though according to him he was an octogenarian). "Why you think I got curly hair?" He would proclaim. There was Javier Guerrero, aka the Latin Lover, their namesake.

(The group of them was known as Guerrero's Posse.) Javier was a thin dark skinned Latino guy who was a ladies' man. Finally, there was Kevin Foster, (also known as "Freeze"), the shooting guard. He along with Jonathan Jenkins (known as JJ) the point guard made up the back court of the team. Their nickname being the run and gun twins. People often said they couldn't tell them apart. Two 5'9 brothers, 150 lbs., medium Afros, same swag, same jive talk. They were inseparable. Even during the summer months, they hung out.

The whole team together calls themselves the AT posse. "We ride together we die together." "I am my brother's keeper", was their motto.

"Where the breezies at, J Dog?" Freeze yells over to JJ as he approaches him from across the Quad. "In the cafeteria." JJ yells back as he gives him dap, a fist pound, and a manly hug. "Well, that's where I be at, you coming dude?" Freeze asks. "Be there in a minute." JJ responds. "I got to go over here to the office and see my counselor, Mr. T. (The name they had for Mr. Thomas.) "Ok bro', holla at you later." Freeze says. The two go their separate ways. Freeze goes to the cafeteria while JJ goes to the office.

As he entered the office, he was asked to have a seat by one of the office secretaries, Ms. Summer, an elderly frail White lady who wore her metal rimmed glasses on her nose. "Wait there." She says pointing to one of the seats in the corner of the room. While he waited, he couldn't help but notice Principal Johnson in a heated argument in his office with a parent. He strained to get the 411 on what was happening. "My son just as smart as the rest of these kids." The lady insisted. The voice came from a thin Black lady, heavy clad in clothing considering the temperature that day was more than seventy-five degrees. She had a high pitched almost squeaky voice and a stare that could stop an elephant in his tracks.

"Well, Ms. Swisher, your son comes from a special education program." "Now if he can't pass the remedial test, we have to put him in the class for special needs pupils." Mr. Johnson replies. "Nonsense." She says pointing to a piece of paper on the table with her long sharp index finger. She says, "Look at his test scores." The young man they talked about stood about 4 feet 9. Small in stature. Couldn't have been more than 110 lbs. wet. And pale. I mean paler than pale. He had a short flaming red Afro with two bald patches on the sides. He was whiter than Da White Boi. Albino. Freckle faced. JJ stood close to Mr. Johnson's office door trying to eavesdrop on what was going on.

"Jenkins," he jumped at the sound of his name being called. Though Mr. Thomas, the resource counselor, had whispered his name, the intensity of him trying to hear what was going on in the principal's office caught him off guard. The silence was broken like a lightning bolt hitting a tree. He jumped to attention at the sound of his name. JJ stood before a round pudgy White man who appeared to be wider than he was tall. He wore a green suit and a black tam. He looked more like an overweight leprechaun than a counselor. "Come on in my office." Mr. Thomas says as he motions JJ to him waving his right hand. Slowly JJ moves towards Mr. Thomas's office. As he entered the office Mr. Thomas motions JJ to have a seat in the chair in front of his desk. Not once did he make eye contact with JJ. He kept reading a folder he held in front of his face and kept making sounds as if he were having a conversation with himself. "Uh hum." "Uh hum. "He kept saying. In between his uh hums were some sporadic "D's." Finally, he looked at JJ. "Son you do plan to go to college don't you?" Mr. Thomas inquires of JJ with his coarse voice. Now the students learned no matter what your intentions were the answer to this question was yes. Otherwise, you would be subjected to an hour-long speech on how you were wasting your potential.

"Yes sir," JJ proclaims. "Well according to your transcripts, you need a math class and a science class." Mr. Thomas informs JJ. "So, I am going to cut two of your electives and add these classes to your transcript." Not wanting to show his disappointment JJ stood up and put a big grin on his face and eagerly said, "Thank you sir," as he shook Mr. Thomas's hand. "Will that be it sir?" JJ asks. "Yes, son that will be it, carry on," Mr. Thomas says. "That boy got a good head on him." JJ heard Mr. Thomas's reply as he scampered out of the office.

JJ wanted to quickly get back outside to Mr. Johnson's office where the little thin Black lady and Mr. Johnson were discussing the weird kids fate. "Amazing", he heard Mr. Johnson say as he approached his office. "Fascinating." He heard Mr. Jackson say as he held a piece of paper in front of his face. By now an array of faculty members were in the office spurting out a bunch of "oohs "and "ah's". "What you think?" Mr. Johnson inquires of Mr. Jackson. "Well, the boy got every answer right on the proficiency exam." "That's gotta be a first." Mr. Jackson replies as he hands the paper back to Mr. Johnson. "Well ma'am I guess you proved your point." "Regular classes for your son." Mr. Johnson says. "Well." The lady says. "Bout time you said something that makes sense." She huffs as she turns to exit. "Come on Benji." The strange looking boy follows her with a stiff gait still twiddling his fingers and making faces.

JJ exits the office and goes towards the quad trying to find Freeze. He spots Freeze under the oak tree in the middle of the campus. "Hey Freeze." JJ yells, getting Freeze's attention. "Hey convict." Freeze replies. "You survived the Warden's office I see." "What Mr. Thomas want?" Freeze inquires of JJ. "Just to change some of my classes around," JJ answers. "Oh," Freeze replies." One of those we want you to reach your full potential speeches, huh?" Freeze says. "Yeah, pretty much." JJ chuckles.

"Hey, you should have seen the dweeb who was in the office, new kid." JJ says. "What new kid?" Freeze asks. Just as he speaks the new kid exits the office with his mother. The sun glistened off his pale skin and his bright red hair looked like it was afire. "That kid over there." JJ says as he points him out. Freeze turns in the direction JJ is pointing. "What the hell?" Freeze exclaims.

For a moment he stared mesmerizing at the funny looking boy. Then a mischievous grin spreads across his face. "You know what I'm thinking?" Freeze says. "No what are you thinking?" JJ replies. Freeze looks at the flagpole nodding his head. First JJ looks at the flagpole indifferently, trying to figure out what Freeze was thinking about. Then he remembers it was a school tradition for the seniors to grab a nerd and hang him on the flagpole on the first day of school. "Oh no." JJ replies. "I don't want no parts of that." "Remember last year." He reminded Freeze. "Some seniors almost got expelled." JJ says. "C'mon now." Freeze says. "It will be fun," Freeze pleads. "Besides the seniors last year were a bunch of dummies." "We gonna get away wit' it easy." Freeze replies. "Look buddy," JJ says. "You on your own on this one." JJ says. "Suit yourself," Freeze replies. "When the first day of school starts, I am going to have some fun." Freeze says. "Suit yourself homie." "I am going to sit this one out." "I can't afford to be expelled." JJ replies. The two high five each other and go their separate ways.

CHAPTER 2

THE CHALLENGE

The next day was Saturday. JJ slept in late. It was about noon when his mother woke him up. "Pookie", his mother's pet name for him. "Get up boy", the little, short plump brown skin lady said shaking him out of his sleep. "Get up boy you got company". She says in her deep contralto voice. JJ sits up on the bed and rubs his eyes, then lay back down and pulls the cover back over himself. "I said get up didn't I." She repeats. This time in a sharp voice. "You got company." She speaks. "Ma", JJ complains. "What I tell you about calling me that in front of my friends." He tells her. "Boy," she replies. "I was in labor with you for 8 hours." "I will call you anything I want", she says as he mouths the words, she says to mock her. "Get up you knock," he heard a familiar voice yell as Freeze came rushing through the door and sat next to JJ on the bed. "Get up boy we got to get our hustle on." Freeze says. "Get up and get your clothes on," he says as he pulls the covers back and swats his friend on the rear end. JJ is laying on his side on his bed in a fetal position clad in his boxers and socks only. "Ok, ok, I'm up," JJ says sitting up on the bed. "Damn, can't a brotha get some sleep around here?" JJ complains. "Nah bruh." Freeze says. "Not as long as it's sick money out there to be landed." "We already missed out on a couple hundred playa." "Now get up P-o-o-k-i-e." Freeze says as he drags out the pronunciation of JJ's pet name his mother has for him purposely so he can irritate his friend. "Alright, I'm up." JJ says as he gets up and sits up on the side of the bed. "And stop calling me that," JJ insists.

"Stop calling you what?" Freeze asks. JJ stares at Freeze with a stern silent stare. "Oh, you mean Pookie," Freeze says with a big grin on his face. JJ remains silent. He just nods with a stoic look on his face. "Pookie, Pookie," Freeze says teasing JJ. JJ begins swinging at Freeze. "You missed, missed again, close that time." Freeze says taunting JJ as he dodges each blow. Finally Freeze tackles JJ on the bed and holds him down.

"Hey, c'mon bruh," Freeze pleads. "Save some of that energy for the B-Ball game." Freeze says. "Get off me, bruh." JJ tells Freeze as he shrugs him off him. JJ gets up and goes to the bathroom, where he brushes his teeth, does a five-minute wash up at the sink, and throws on some shorts, a tee shirt, some socks, and tennis shoes. He was already to go in 15 minutes.

Both set out for the neighborhood park. "So, what's the plan man?" Freeze says to JJ. "I don't know?" "What's the plan?" "You the perky one with all the energy." JJ replies. "OK, way I see it, we bet everything we got when we play Ray Ray and Stimpy." "They never beat us." "Same thing with Lil Z and Malcolm." "Then when we play Big Baby and Slim, we bet half." "We haven't beaten them yet." Freeze strategizes. The two agree with this plan.

Through the first two games they stick with their plan and double their money. About time they finished the first two games they had won two hundred dollars. Now it was time for the game against Big Baby and Slim. They only bet half of what they have left. Big Baby and Slim were totally opposite of each other. Slim was a light skin brother with wavy hair, about 5'9". Slender build. He was the smack talker of the two. Big Baby was low key, stood about 6'5" and was a dark skin brother with a close-cut hairdo and had a muscular build like a Black Adonis. He was the quiet one of the two. "We betting a hundred." JJ says as he threw in a wad of balled up $20s in the pot. "A hundred it is." Slim confirms as he counts and straightens out five $20 bills and adds them to the pot. True to form Slim begins his smack talk before the game gets started. He knew Freeze's weakness was his pride. "Oh, I understand y'all "scared." Slim professed. "Why don't y'all bet the whole two hunned'?" Silence from Freeze and JJ. "Y'all know y'all gonna lose, huh?" "I understand." "Playing it safe." Slim says as he continues to agitate.

"Naw we not gonna lose." Freeze says as Slim finally got under his skin. "Here, the whole two hundred duckets." "Y'all going down." Freeze proclaims as he throws the other hundred on the pile.

"What you doing man?" JJ whispers as Freeze walks back towards him. "No worries dude," Freeze assures JJ. "I got this." Freeze adds. "We going to 24 by twos, got to win by 4." Freeze says as he turns back and talks to Slim. "Winners take out." Freeze adds. "That's fine with me." Slim says. They look at JJ. JJ remains silent. He just nods in agreement. "Here y'all take the ball first seeing this the last time y'all gone touch the ball." Slim says laughing. "We will be shirts, y'all be skins," Slim adds.

JJ and Freeze take their shirts off and threw them to the side of the court. JJ started off the game passing the ball into Freeze. For the next 30 minutes they played a fierce game in which the lead changed hands a couple times. With the scores Shirts 22 Skins 20, Freeze had the ball. He was dribbling the ball in the far-right corner with Slim guarding him. Once again Slim plays to Freeze's ego. "Shoot the ball, you scared?" Slim challenges Freeze. The two had been trash talking the whole game. "The only thing I'm scared of is yo mama". Freeze lashes out. When Freeze stops dribbling, he stands in the far-right hand corner of the court.

"Shoot the ball," Slim yells to Freeze "You scared?" "No pass the ball." JJ says. "That's not your shot." JJ reminds Freeze. "Yeah, that's what I thought." "You scared to shoot the ball." Slim eggs Freeze on. "Look I will even give you some room." Slim yells after he steps back a few steps from Freeze. "Show me what you working wit'." Slim challenges Freeze as Freeze squares up to shoot the ball.

"N-O-O!" JJ yells as the ball flies out of Freeze's hands. It appears the ball was moving in slow motion as it made its way to the hoop. As the ball reaches the hoop it appeared to go halfway in then pops out. Big Baby grabs the rebound over a shorter JJ, clears the key and quickly turns back towards the basket and slam dunks the ball over JJ.

"Game over." Slim yells as he does his victory dance making his hands like guns shooting in the air. He walks over to pick up the pile of $20s sitting at the foot of the basketball pole that were weighed down by JJ's T-shirt. Freeze walks towards Slim in an aggressive manner with his fists balled up. "Man, you hustled us."

Freeze protests. "Don't be mad bro'." Slim says as he walks over to pick up the 20's. "That there is part of the game." Slim says with a smile on his face. Freeze corners Slim and hems him up by the collar holding him against the basketball pole. "C'mon man." Slim pleads. "We won fair and square." "Hey homie be cool." JJ says as he intercedes with Freeze and Slim before the incident gets out of hand. "C'mon it ain't worth it bruh." JJ says as he pulls Freeze back. Slim begins distributing the funds he has picked up with Big Baby. He goes back to Freeze and hands him a $20. "No bad feelings my brother." Slim says in his smooth voice as he hands Freeze a $20 bill. Freeze snatches the $20 bill out of Slims hand, balls it up and throws it on to the middle of the court. Slim backs away from Freeze with both hands up in a conciliatory manner and turns towards JJ.

"You gotta do something 'bout that temper of yo' boy." Slim says as he extends his hand to shake JJs hand. Slim stands there with his hand extended for a minute as JJ stands staring him down arms folded refusing to shake hands. Slim slowly withdraws his hand. He motions his hand back across his wavy hair and tells JJ as he walks away looking over his shoulder tauntingly saying, "Hey potna dude, don't go away mad," he says laughing. Then he says, "Just go away."

Big Baby counts his share of the winnings then comes over and to shake JJ's hand. "Good game, bro," he says as the two embrace each other. Big Baby goes over to shake Freeze's hand. "Good game, homie." Big Baby says to Freeze. Freeze still steaming mad didn't respond. Big Baby holds his hand out for a few seconds, then pats Freeze on the shoulder and walks off.

Both JJ and Freeze just stood there on the basketball court for about 3 minutes in silence. Finally, JJ spoke. "You ought not treat Big Baby like that." "He's a cool dude." JJ says. "I know", Freeze agrees. "I was just mad at that asshole Slim."

Another moment of silence goes by . JJ breaks the silence again. "Now we broke." JJ complains. "Man, we should of took them." Freeze says. "Yeah, if you would have passed the ball." JJ complains. "Oh, it's my fault." Freeze says. "What happened to we win as a team; we lose as a team?"

Another moment of silence goes by. JJ once again breaks the silence. "Yeah, you right homie." "No finger pointing." JJ says. Again, a moment of silence as the only sound that could be heard was the traffic going by.

"Yeah, you right, it was my fault." "I should've passed it." "I let my pride get to me." Freeze says. "That's okay." JJ responds. Freeze says, "We will get them next time." "You notice this the closest we came to beating them in a long time." "Yeah." JJ, says shaking his head. "We getting better, huh.""

C'mon." JJ says. 'I will treat you to lunch." "Ha." Freeze replies. "With what?" "We both broke." A moment of silence then both simultaneous look toward the middle of the court where the balled up $20 still lay. Both jump up and race towards it. They both dive for it at the same time. And end up laying sprawled out on the basketball court. JJ reaches it first.

They both sit up laughing. "Getting slow in your old age, huh old man?" JJ says teasing Freeze. "Ok, you win." Freeze concedes. "I am at your mercy." JJ says. "We ride together." Freeze says. "We die together." And they both say in unison, "I am my brother's keeper. "Then they do a funny handshake.

"C'mon, we can split it." JJ says. "Ok, homie." Freeze says. The two set off from the park passing the basketball back and forth to each other taking turns dribbling the basketball as they headed on their way to the burger place.

CHAPTER 3

THE PRANK

JJ was up early Monday morning. For most kids, the first day of school was a drag. But for a jock, especially a senior jock, you were like royalty. "Good morning son." Momma says as JJ comes down the stairs. "You up early this morning." "See you got those clothes on I bought you." She tells him. "C'mon stand here so I can check you out." His mother says.

"C'mon, Ma." JJ complains as she fixes his collar. "Now, you know momma gotta make sure you looking proper baby for your first day as a senior," She says. "C'mon, Ma." JJ says again. "I am not a baby no mo'." He tells her. "Hush boy." She says primping his clothes and fixing his collar as he makes faces and grunts of disapproval. She stands back and says, "Now you gonna always be my baby, son, you hear?" she says. "Yeah, Ma." He says under his breath.

"You need a ride to school?" She offers him with a big grin on her face. "No, Ma, yo' lil baby can walk." He says sarcastically in a baby voice. "Ma, I am starting my senior year in high school, not kindergarten." He points out to her. "Okay, baby." "Give mama a kiss," she says. He gives his mother a peck on the cheek then he was off to school.

He walks briskly away from the house until he was out of sight of his mother. He then quickly takes off the clothing his mother had bought him revealing the beige Dickey's and red polo shirt he had under the clothes he was wearing. He stuffed the clothes he had on in his backpack. After switching clothes, he scurried off to school.

When he got on campus, he notices a crowd gathered at the Quad in the middle of the campus. There was a lot of joking and laughter going on. As he approaches, he saw amongst the crowd laughing harder than anyone was Freeze.

"What's so funny?" He inquired of his friend as he approaches him. Freeze answers, "Dude." He spurted out between his laughter. He greets JJ with a high five. "You late dude," he says trying to control his laughter. "What?" JJ asks. "You missed out on the fun." "Look." Freeze says. Pointing towards the flagpole in the right corner of the Quad.

There hanging from the flagpole a human body. It was the pale weird looking kid. "Momma!" The weird kid yells. "Momma!" The crowd mocks him.

"Ain't that the funniest thing you ever seen." Freeze proclaims. "The funniest thing." JJ repeats half-heartedly because he was not really feeling this joke. "Momma!" The boy yells again. His underwear showed as the hook from the flagpole rope bungled his blue underwear into a wedgie. His pants were down to his ankles now and his shirt covers his pale face. "Momma!" He yells again.

This time the rope had rotated him facing the crowd. His shirt had fallen to the ground. You could see the tears streaming down from his face. Somehow JJ did not see the humor in this prank anymore.

"Ok, Freeze that's enough." JJ says to Freeze. "Let him down." "Momma!" The poor boy moans again. By this time, a mob had gathered around and some of the most raucous people had started pelting objects at him. "You want him down, dude?" Freeze says to JJ as he pelts the boy with wood chips that underline the trees on campus. "Let him down yourself." Freeze says. JJ stood there a minute in silence watching the crowd taunt the boy. Everything seems to be happening in slow motion. "Momma," the boy calls out again.

"OK, I will let him down." JJ says as he moves toward the rope bound to the flagpole. The crowd begins to "Boo" as JJ begins to untie the rope. "Hater." Someone says as JJ slowly takes the knot out of the rope.

First the crowd was in a big uproar. Then there came a sudden hush. JJ was so intrigued in getting the knot out of the rope he did not notice the person that comes up behind him. A hand comes from behind him and lands on his shoulder. JJ shrugs the hand off without looking behind him. Again the hand comes on his shoulder. "No." JJ says in response to the hand on his shoulder. "Enough is enough." JJ says. The hand pats him on the shoulder again. "I'm not trying to hear you." JJ responds as he continues to work on the knot in the rope. This time the person behind him turns him around. To his surprise he was now facing Mr. Jackson.

He took a big swallow. It felt like his heart fell down to his feet. "I-I -I- d-d." He stammers trying to deny any guilt. "To my office," a sterned faced Mr. Jackson says pointing his huge hand towards the office. JJ trudged slowly to the office. "Get him down," Mr. Jackson orders the mob. About five people seem to rush to get the boy down upon Mr. Jackson's command.

Mr. Jackson was an imposing man. He stood about six feet four and weighs a solid two hundred fifty pounds. But at this time to JJ, he appeared to be an eight feet tall monster. JJ arrives at the office door and waits for Mr. Jackson to open the door.

"Have a seat boy." Mr. Jackson commands with authority. You could tell when Mr. Jackson was angry with you. Not by his stoic mannerisms but how he addressed you. If you were addressed as son, or young man, chances are you were in his good graces. But if you were addressed as boy, chances are you were in deep trouble.

Mr. Jackson calls over the intercom to Ms. Summers. "Bring me suspension papers, please." JJ sinks down in his chair. Mr. Jackson sits there filling out some papers. He hands a copy of the papers to JJ. "OK young man." Mr. Jackson says. "Take these papers home and have your mother sign them." "She and I will have a conference soon." Mr. Jackson says. JJ takes the papers from Mr. Jackson. He grabs his book bag and walks out the office and starts walking to the bus stop.

It took forever, it seems, to get to the bus stop. He got there just as a bus was leaving. He tries to flag it down, but it was too late. The bus had already pulled off without him. He drops his book bag at his feet. "Man, this has been some day." He thought." "What else could go wrong?" He thinks. Just then five-o pulls up. "Great," JJ says as the officer steps out of his car. As he approaches JJ, JJ put his hands up in the air above his head. "Son, you've been watching too much TV." The officer says. The officer tells JJ, "Put your hands down son." JJ slowly puts his hands down.

The officer is a tall White guy. Clean shaven. Average height and weight. Looks to be in his late 20s early 30s. JJ speaks. "How are you doing, Officer?" JJ asks the officer. "I'm doing mighty fine, young man," the officer responds. "Little early to be out of school?" The officer asks JJ. JJ begins to reach in his book bag then he stops and looks at the gun in the officer's holster. "I have papers in my book bag." JJ tells the officer. The officer nods his approval for JJ to go in his book bag. JJ reaches into his book bag and pulls out his suspension papers.

He hands the papers to the officer. The officer looks over the paper. The officer hands the papers back to JJ. "First day of school and suspended, huh son." The officer says. "Yeah, officer,"JJ responds. "But I'm a good kid, Officer." JJ says. "Yeah, I know kid." The officer says. "Let me guess, you didn't do it?" He asks JJ anticipating his excuse. "Really, Officer, I really didn't do it." JJ responds. "You know how many times I hear that story, son?" The officer asks JJ. "Probably 1,000,000 times." JJ says. JJ says. "But I am the one outta of 1 million who is telling you the truth." JJ tells the officer.

The officer looks straight at JJ. Then he says, "Somehow I believe you, son." "I've been there where you are, son." He goes on to say. "I know it seems tough now, but you'll get over it." "Really." JJ says. "You mean you've been suspended before?" JJ asks. "Of course, I have." "I haven't been wearing a badge all of my life." The officer says.

"What were you suspended for?" JJ asks. "I'm not going to go into detail." The officer tells JJ. "Let's say it had to do with some girls." Then the officer looks at JJ and asks, "Did yours have to do with girls?" The officer asks JJ. JJ shakes his head from side to side to indicate "no". Now the officer shakes his head. "See, son." The officer says. "If you gonna get in trouble you got to be smart about it." "My suspension was almost worth it." The officer says with a big grin on his face. JJ laughs. "You have a good day, son." The officer tells JJ. "Goodbye, officer." JJ says. "You have a good day too, sir." JJ says. The officer gets back in his car and drives off.

JJ sits at the bus stop pondering his dilemma. "First day of school and suspended." "Got to get home and erase those messages on the phone before mom gets home." He thinks as he waits on the bus. "You riding young man?" A deep hoarse voice blurts out. He was so caught up in his thoughts he did not notice the bus pull up. He looks up to see a heavy set bearded White man sporting his khaki brown uniform speaking to him. "You riding or what Buddy?" The man says again. "I got a schedule to keep now." "Ain't got all day." He tells JJ. JJ slowly gets up and steps on the bus. He shows the bus driver his pass and goes to the back of the bus.

About five minutes into the bus ride. The bus driver calls back to JJ. "Suspended from school, huh?" JJ looks surprised. "What is it with these old people." "They psychic or what?" JJ asks himself. JJ answers, "Yes sir." "But I didn't do it." The driver answers, "Yes, boy." "That's everybody's story." "That was my story when I got suspended from school." The bus driver says. "You got suspended from school?" JJ asks. "Yes, I got suspended from school young man." The driver answers.

"Wow," JJ thinks. First a police officer and now a bus driver. JJ was beginning to think that getting suspended from school was a rite of passage. "What you get suspended for?" JJ asks the bus driver. "My crime was graffiti." The driver says.

The two were quiet for a few minutes. Then the bus driver says to JJ, "Answer me this question?" The driver asks JJ. "The incident that happened, could you have prevented it from happening?" JJ thought about the question the driver had asked. JJ answers, "Yes, I probably could have." The bus driver says, "Well, son, that makes you as guilty as the perpetrator." JJ sits quietly and thinks about what the driver has said to him. "I want you to sit and marinate on that for the rest of the ride." The driver tells JJ.

Each moment that passes by JJ was trying to think of an alibi on why he was suspended. On what seems like a forever bus trip he finally reaches his stop. "I'm getting off here sir." JJ tells the bus driver. He took a deep breath as he exited the bus. "You have a nice day young man." The bus driver says. "Keep your head up." He says, trying to encourage JJ. "Thank you, sir," JJ says as he gets off the bus. He stands and watches the bus till it is out of sight. Slowly he turns and walks meticulous down the street like a convicted man walking towards the gallows.

As he nears his home, he could see a woman in a blue dress with a red head scarf tied around her hair standing on the porch with her arms folded. "Too late to erase the message," he thinks. "She already knows." As he got closer, he could see the fire in her eyes and the serious scowl on her face. He walks up on the porch. He looks at his mother's face. The expression on her face does not change. She does not say a word. She just points towards the door motioning him to enter the house. He enters the house slowly and he waits in the corridor for his mother to enter. She stands motionless on the porch for about 5 minutes. Then she slowly enters the house. Again, without talking she motions for JJ to sit on the couch.

He removes his book bag and sets it on the floor. He sits down slowly on the couch. His mother comes and sits on the couch on the opposite side of the room. She sits silently staring into space. Again, she remains silent. The tension in the air was thicker than mud on a cold winter night. The silence was almost deafening.

Finally, JJ decides to break the silence. "But Ma." "I did..." She puts her hand up to halt his speech. Again, there is silence. After about another 5 minutes she speaks. "Hand me that cell phone," she orders him. He went into his backpack to grab his phone. "But Ma", he tries to explain before he hands the phone over. This time she put her finger in front of her mouth cutting him off as she shook her head back and forth. She motions for him to hand over the phone. He hands her the phone.

"Now," she whispers, "Go to your room." "I don't want to see you no more today." She tells him. He slowly begins to ascend the stairs. "And take that video game out of your room." She orders him to do.

He turns around, "C'mon, Ma," he pleads. "Don't c'mon Ma me boy", she says pointing him up the stairs. "And no dinner for you tonight." She informs him. He huffs as he reaches the entrance to his room.

First he sits on his bed. "Video game," he hears his mother's voice ring out. He looks towards the tv in the corner of his room. He storms towards the tv and snatches the video game off the top. Begrudgingly he unplugs it, storms towards the entrance of his bedroom and lays the game outside his door. He stomps back to his bed and plops on it. "You need to get rid of that attitude boy," his mother yells up the stairs. He takes a deep breath and sighs. "You hear me boy, don't let me have to come up there." She threatens. "Alright, Ma," he answers. "And no dinner for you tonight," she adds. "OK Ma, I got it, no dinner." He sits at the end of his bed staring at the wall.

At the corner of his eye he spots a magazine. He gets out of bed to grab the magazine. He calls downstairs to his mother and sarcastically says with a smirk on his face, "Can I read a magazine?" His mother answers him. "Jonathan Jeffries Jenkins." "Don't you get smart with me, boy." "Do you want me to come up there?" She speaks. "Uh oh." He thinks. "This is serious," She calls him by all three of his names. Last time she did that she almost blew a gasket. "You hear me boy?" she says. "You want me to come up these stairs?" She says as he hears her beginning to come up the stairs. "No, Ma." he answers. "It's cool, Ma." "Please, don't come upstairs, Ma." He pleads. He hears her stop and go back downstairs.

"Woo." He says, "That was close." He could hear her say, "Don't play with me boy." "I brought you into this world and I'll take you out." He picks up a magazine with a guy dressed in a basketball uniform with a basketball in his hands. He grabs the magazine and lays down on his belly on his bed. He begins thumbing through the magazine. "Now that's going to be me," he says pointing to one of the players in the magazine with a smile on his face. "NBA bound," he brags.

He continues to thumb through the magazine, till he falls asleep. He was awakened about three hours later to a gentle voice calling his name. "J. J. wake up baby." The voice says. First, he thought he was dreaming. He sits up straight in the bed and rubs the sleep out of his eyes. As his eyes begin to focus a brown skin woman begins to appear before him. She holds a tray of food with a glass of milk. "Here baby, Momma got you some spaghetti." She says l. He blinks his eyes once more, then grabs the tray which has a plate of spaghetti and a glass of milk on it.

His mother turns and exits the room. He has lost count the times his mother has sent him to bed without dinner only to bring him something to eat later. "Say your blessing, baby," she tells him. "Yeah, Ma," he answers her. He says a quick blessing then begins chowing down the food. Then he falls back asleep.

CHAPTER 4

JJ'S PUNISHMENT

"Jay-Jay." A drowsy JJ hears his mother's voice call as she shakes him from a deep sleep. "Get up boy."
She demanded still shaking him. "Alright, Ma. I'm up stop shaking me, please," he replies as he sits up
on the edge of his bed. "Boy don't you sass me," she says as she gives him a quick slap upside his head.
"Ow Ma," he says. "Dang, sorry, Ma, I said please." he says. "Oh, you gone be sorry," she replies. "Here I
am missing a half day's work because you acting foolish at school." She tells him. "Ma, I tried to tell you it
wasn't me." JJ says. "What you say boy? "You talking back?" She asks him as she walks towards him with
her hand up again. "No, Ma." "I'm not talking back." He says as he puts his hands up to protect his face.
"Please, Ma put your 45s back in the holster," he says.

She steps away from him and continues to rant and rave on as she left the room. JJ got up and goes
to the bathroom. He did a quick wash up and brushes his teeth. All the while he could hear his mother
fussing about losing a day's work. He pays little attention to her rambling; he has other things on his mind.
Right now, he is going to the principal's office. "Two weeks suspension." He thinks. "I can live with that."
After all it was September. Basketball season didn't start till November. It was the second consequence
that worries him. Getting kicked off the basketball team.

He finishes brushing his teeth and steps into his bedroom. He lays his clothes out on the bed. Just as
he undresses out of his pjs his mother comes busting through the door.

"Boy you need to hurry up here and stop taking your time." She tells JJ. JJ stood up covering his
unclad body with the clothes he had laid out on the bed. "Ma," he protests. "I don't have no clothes on."
He informs her. His mother crosses her arms and looks over the rim of her glasses and states, "Boy I used
to change your diaper." "You ain't got nothing I ain't seen and nothing I want to see." "Now get your
clothes on and let's go. "She tells him. "Alright, Ma, give me some privacy, please." He requests. "Lil JJ
not Lil JJ anymore." He tells her. "There's been some alterations down there since you last changed my
diaper." He says with a smirk on his face. His mother smacks him one upside the head. "Ow, Ma." He says
in reaction to her popping him upside the head. "Boy don't you joke with me at a time like this." She tells
him. "Alright, alright Ma, sorry." "Be cool with that right hook of yours," he says rubbing the left side of his

head. "Man," he tells her. "You ought to get that right hook of yours registered." He says joking around. "Are you still joking around," she says in a stern voice. "No ma'am." He says as he straightens his face up taking the smile off of it looking serious. "I'm getting dressed now." He tells her.

His mother steps out the room, still talking to herself. JJ finishes getting dressed. After he brushes his hair he throws on some deodorant and heads down the stairs. "Here is a breakfast sandwich for you," she says as she hands him a sandwich and a cup of juice. "You can eat it in the car," she tells him. "Man, this really must've been serious." He thinks. "Man, she was letting him eat in the car was like cussing in church," he thought. That like never happens.

He and his mother exit the house towards a red Volvo parked in the driveway. From there they were off to his school. From the time they left the house till the time they got in the car his mother was fussing about everything from JJ shaming the family to JJ getting suspended from school to JJ not taking the trash out.

Everything she said went over his head. Only things he could think of was if he was going to get kicked off the football and basketball teams. "Get out the car boy," his mother screamed. He was so caught up in his thoughts he did not realize they have pulled up in front of the school. JJ slowly gets out the car. His mother sits in the driver seat waiting for him to open the car door for her. He runs around from the passenger side to the driver side to open her car door.

The walk from the parking lot to the principal's office was like the last walk of a condemned man walking to the gallows. Finally, the trek to the principal's office ended. JJ stood at the office door. "Uh hum", his mom hinted for him to open the door for her. JJ opens the door for his mother. As they stepped into the office, they come face to face with Ms. Summers one of the school secretaries. She greets them. "Good morning Ms. Jenkins." Ms. Summers says. JJ's mother says nothing. She just nods her head. "Mr. Johnson will be with you shortly." Miss Summers says. Both JJ and his mother took a seat. His mother grabs a magazine that was on the table.

Finally, Mr. Johnson enters the main office. He walks over to the secretary. "You got any mail for me, Ms. Summers?" He asks her. She hands him some papers then whispers something in his ear as she points towards JJ and his mother. Principal Johnson walks over to the two of them and introduces himself. "Hello ma'am, I am Mr. Johnson." "Could you step in my office?" He says as he leads the two to his office.

"Have a seat," he says as he directs them to two chairs in front of his desk. "Now Mr. Jenkins, what do you have to say for yourself?" He asks JJ. JJ went on to explain how he had walked up on the scene and that actually he was helping the boy, not hazing him."

Well, Mr. Jenkins, the vice principal, says different." Principal Johnson says. "Ms. Jenkins you have anything to say?" Mr. Johnson says. "Well sir," she says, "When I first heard about this I was highly upset with my son." "But after I hear my son's side of the story, I believe him." "My son does not lie to me and he is a good kid." She adds. JJ sits up proudly in his seat. That was the first time he heard his mother talk about him like that.

"Well unfortunately, Ms. Jenkins our vice principal says different." "We frown upon this type of behavior." "Hazing is a very serious offense." "I have no other choice but to suspend your son for two weeks." Mr. Johnson informs her. "Well at least I am still on the football and basketball team," JJ thinks.

Mr. Jackson steps in the office. He looks towards JJ and his mother. "So, this is the young man with the hazing incident, huh?" Mr. Jackson says. "What are the consequences?" Mr. Jackson inquires. "Two weeks suspended." Mr. Johnson informs Mr. Jackson. "Oh no." Mr. Jackson says. "That's just a slap on the wrist." "Last year we expelled a couple of students for this kind of behavior." "Isn't he on the football and basketball team?" Mr. Jackson inquires. Everyone nods. JJ gulps and takes a deep breath in anticipation of the next words coming out of Mr. Jackson's mouth. "Well, I think he ought to be kicked off both teams." Mr. Jackson insists.

JJ felt like a dagger had been thrust through his heart. "Damn, off the football and basketball teams." He thinks. "That was the only purpose for coming to school." JJ thinks. "Man, I wonder if I am off the baseball team, too?" Then he thinks, "I dare not ask." "Don't want to put no ideas in their heads." "I will cross that river when we get to it."

First JJ sinks down disappointingly in his seat. Then he hears the voice of his coach, Mr. Smith in his head saying, "Never show your opponent your weakness." At hearing these words, he quickly sat up in his seat. He tries to look cool but inside he was devastated. It took all of his bravado to keep from crying. ".

Now, Mr. Jackson." JJ's mother says. "My son was counting on getting a basketball scholarship to get into college." His mother says. If there was a silver lining in this situation it was hearing his mother stick up for him. "Well, Ms. Jenkins, I have to agree with Mr. Jackson." "Our student athletes have to be role models in this school." Mr. Johnson says. "So as of now, Mr. Jenkins you are suspended from the football and basketball teams."

JJ thinks, "Wow, why not just give me the electric chair." Mrs. Jenkins stands up abruptly. "I think this is so unfair," she says. "Come on, JJ," she says as she summons JJ. As she exits the office she turns back towards Mr. Johnson, "This is not the last you will see of me," she says sharply as they exit.

The both of them head for the parking lot. JJ's mom is fuming. Talking to herself as she usually does when she is upset. "This time," he thinks. "Least she not mad at me." They arrive to the car. Mom stands at the car door. "Uh hum". A hint for JJ to open the car door for her. JJ runs around from the passenger door to the driver side door and opens the door for his mother. They both sit in the car. For a moment they both sat in silence. JJ speaks.

"Thanks, Ma," he says. She looks at him puzzled. "Thanks for what son?" She inquires. "Thanks for believing in me." JJ says. "Oh baby," she replies. "You don't have to thank me for doing the right thing." "One thing I know, my baby don't lie to me." She tells him. A moment of silence. Then his mother says, "Except that time you stole those cupcakes out the cupboard." They look at each other and start laughing.

"Ma," he blurts out between laughs. "I was four years old then." He informs her. "I know baby," she adds. "Standing there with cupcake all over your face denying you took the cupcakes." They laugh again.

As their laughter subsides JJ looks at his mom and says, "Seeing you in action today was worth getting those two right hooks upside my head." "Oh, I'm sorry baby." His mother says, "I just want the best for you." "Mama didn't hurt you, did she?" She asks him. "Naw, Ma," JJ says. "You know it takes more than that to get through that thick skull of mine." He tells her. They sit back and laugh again. They sit there quietly for a minute. Then JJ says, "Give me a wet one right here," pointing to his left cheek. His mother looks at him in surprise. "Oh," she says. "You mean it's not embarrassing for Momma to give her boy a kiss in public?" "Naw, Ma," he says as he encourages her. "Give it up to yo lil Pookie, some love." His mother lays a kiss on his cheek. "Love ya, Ma." he says. "Love ya son." She responds. They both just sit in the car for a few moments just enjoying each other's company.

CHAPTER 5

JJ'S REDEMPTION

Normally two weeks out of school would be like a vacation. These two weeks were like being incarcerated. And there was no sneaking out of the house. Nosy Ms. Harris on one side of their house and nosy Mama Jewel on the other side.

"Damn do they ever sleep." JJ thinks to himself. Though Momma came to the conclusion JJ did no wrong she still did not want him in the streets all day. "Too much trouble out there," she would say.

It wasn't a total loss though. Momma did allow JJ to have his tv and video games back. But now it was Monday morning. Two weeks had gone by. First day back to school. Finally bailing out of this prison it seems. Back to school today. Nothing to look forward to. No football, no basketball, no scholarship.

"Damn." "All because I'm trying to do a good deed." "Never again." He thought. "No more mister nice guy." He thinks. He gets up slowly. He went through his usual daily routine. He sat up on his bed clad in his white boxer underwear. He sat there for about 5 minutes and let out a big yawn and stretch.

"Hmm," he thinks. "Where is Ma?" "She would usually be up here by now bugging me to get up." He thought. "Ma," he calls out. She doesn't answer. "Mama," he yells. Still no answer. He slowly gets up. He starts his morning routine. He lays his clothes out on his bed. He takes a quick wash off, brushes his teeth and gets dressed.

"Mama", he calls again. No answer. He begins to search the house room to room. "Mama." Still no answer. He goes downstairs. He looks in the kitchen. There is a note on the kitchen table. He picks it up. It is in his mother's handwriting. "Left your breakfast in the microwave oven," the note reads. He looks in the microwave oven. There sat a green plate with some scrambled eggs and finger sausages.

He warms the plate up in the microwave. He took a bottle of orange juice out the refrigerator as his food warms up. He looks for a cup in the cupboard. He can't find one. He begins drinking out the bottle of OJ after he couldn't find a cup.

"Ding." The microwave bell goes off. He retrieves his plate. He almost dropped it because it was so hot. He didn't bother to sit down or get eating utensils. He begins chowing down his food using his hands.

He chases down the food with what was left in the bottle of OJ. He gathers his bookbag then leaves out the door off to school.

He decides to walk to school instead of riding the bus. The long walk will do a lot to refresh his mind. The trek to school was a tedious journey. The whole time he walks, he ponders on how boring it was going to be without football and basketball this year. He finally made it to school. He plods up the stairs. He doesn't notice the other students buzzing around him. He barely notices the person walking up behind him.

"Mr. Jenkins," he jumps as he is startled by the voice that has come from behind him. He turns to face a short stocky pale faced blonde man. He was about five feet tall and five feet wide. Looks like he was a court jester the way he was dressed in a polka dot shirt and bright red pants and the toes of his red shoes appeared to curl up to the sky. He looks so round it looks like you could just roll him down the hallway. It was Mr. Garrett, the hall monitor. "Mr. Jenkins," he says again in his deep voice. "Yeah, Mr. Garret." JJ answers. "You are wanted in the office son," he says as he points down the hall with his fat stubby index finger. "Yes sir," JJ says. He looks down the hall and stares for about a minute. He plods down the hallway towards the principal's office. "What now," he thought. He has been in the principal's office more time this month than all of his entire high school stay. He enters the office. Ms. Mills, one of the school secretaries, greets him.

"Good morning." "Mr. Jenkins,"she says. "Have a seat till Mr. Johnson calls for you," she tells him.

Miss Mills is a petite little lady. Every boy in school wants to get a look at Miss Mills in the office. She was stacked like hotcakes on a Sunday morning breakfast platter. Always walking around in those short sexy skirts showing off her fine body and her low low-cut blouses showing more cleavage than the bedrock of a mountain top rock quarry. There she was flaunting herself around the office with her halter top and a mini skirt. For a minute JJ was so entrenched in watching her he has forgotten what he came to the office for.

JJ looks towards Mr. Johnson's office. He strains to see through the glass that was lined with wires. He made out Mr. Johnson, his mother, coach Smith, the goofy kid and the goofy kid's mother. JJ thought, "What my mother doing here?" "I thought she was at work?" He takes a deep breath. "What now," he thought as he sighs. JJ sat twiddling his thumbs and fidgeting around, anxiously at what was next.

"Mr. Jenkins, enter please," Mr. Johnson says. JJ enters Mr. Johnson's office. He stands at the office door. "Have a seat, Mr. Jenkins." Mr. Johnson says. JJ comes into the office and has a seat. JJ sits in a chair in the corner. He looks up to meet the eyes of his mother. It appears all eyes are on him.

"Well Mr. Jenkins we are here to discuss your status at this school," Mr. Johnson says. JJ looks at his mother whose arms were folded, and stare was stern. JJ does not have a clue as to what is going on. "So first we have agreed among us you owe Mr. Swisher and his mother an apology." Mr. Johnson says. "But" JJ answers. "But I, uh, ..." "Uhm" his mother says cutting him off with that deadly stare of hers. He took a deep breath and sighs.

JJ turns to the funny looking boy and his mother. Again, he sighs. "Ms." He pauses and looks at the principal, "Swisher," the principal says. "Ms. Swisher and uh," again he pauses and looks at the principal, "and Benjamin" Mr. Johnson says. "And Benjamin, I apologize for my behavior." JJ says. "And it won't happen again." JJ's mother adds. He looks at his mother. She gives him that look. He turns back to the two of them. And he adds, "And it won't happen again," JJ says.

"You ought to be ashamed of yourself." The boy's mother exclaimed as she pointed her stubby finger towards him. "Yes, ma'am." JJ replies.

"Miss Swisher could you leave us alone now." Mr. Johnson requests. The lady grabs the funny looking boy by the hand and exits the office. She glares back at JJ and rolls her eyes before she leaves the office.

"Now for you Mr. Jenkins." Mr. Johnson says. "Your mother and I and coach Smith have worked out a deal so that you can still play basketball." JJ looks at Coach Smith and Coach Smith nods. Mr. Johnson explains. "You still want to play football and basketball don't you," he asks JJ. "Why yes sir," JJ says as he perks up in his seat. "You Mr. Jenkins can play football and basketball on one condition." Mr. Johnson says. "Yes sir," JJ responds. "Anything sir." JJ eagerly says. Mr. Johnson says, "That you show Benjamin around campus his first month here." Mr. Johnson says.

"Show Benjamin around campus for a month?" JJ repeats. "Yes," Mr. Johnson says. "He is new to this environment and needs someone of your stature and influence to guide him. This way you will only be suspended two football games and when the basketball season starts you will be able to start every game in basketball, pending you don't get into any more trouble." Mr. Johnson says.

JJ looks at his mother with a puzzled look. "You heard what the man said." His mother says forcefully. "You have to show Benjamin around for a month." She repeats. "Thank the man," she adds.

JJ took a deep breath and said, "Thank you, Mr. Johnson." "Well, if the both of you have no other questions, I believe we are done here." Mr. Johnson says. "Thank you, Mr. Johnson." JJs mother says. "Thank you and your son." Mr. Johnson says. JJs mother stares at him. Then gives him the evil eye. "Oh, thank you, Mr. Johnson." JJ adds in a dry tone.

JJ slowly left the office with his mother. She gives him a quick peck on the cheek and is on her way off to work. As he leaves and exits the door, he sees a ruckus over on the south side of the school near the basketball courts.

As he gets closer, he notices Freeze throwing something. There was a crowd cheering him on. In the middle of the crowd stood Benjamin. Freeze was hitting him with water balloons. Each time a balloon hit Benjamin the crowd would cheer. JJ walks up behind Freeze as he rears back to throw another balloon. JJ grabs his hand with the balloon in it before he could throw it.

Freeze turns to see JJ. "Hey, pal, you want to join in on the fun?" Freeze asks. JJ just stands there staring at Freeze. "OK, get your own balloon," Freeze tells JJ pointing to a blue milk crate full of water balloons. Freeze winds back again to throw a balloon. This time JJ knocks the balloon out of his hand.

A hush grows among the crowd. Freeze faces JJ startled for a minute. He looks JJ in the eyes and reads the fury in his face. For a minute he stares silently. Then he speaks, "What the hell has gotten into you?" Freeze asks JJ. JJ grabs Freeze by the collar and pulls him so close their noses are almost touching.

"That's enough!" JJ yells. Freeze forcefully pulls away from JJ and adjusts his collar. "You trippin' man." Freeze replies. "You taking up for this freak over your lifetime bud?" "Whatever happened to one for all and all for one? Ride together till we die." "You going to take up for this retard over me, your lifelong friend?" Freeze says. "Oh yeah one for all and all for one." "Ride together till we Die." JJ repeats this slogan. "Let's see where did that end?" He continues. "Oh yeah," JJ finishes. "That ended between you leaving me holding the rope at the flagpole and Mr. Jackson suspending me for two weeks." "You left me hanging, bruh." JJ says. "I mean where you been the last two weeks?" "No phone calls, didn't come by the house." "What's up?" JJ says.

"Ok, that's how you feel, suit yourself." Freeze says. "You want to be the savior for this retard, go ahead." "Our friendship is over." Freeze says as he storms off.

JJ says. "Fine with me." "I don't need no backstabbing friend like you anyway," JJ yells back. He looks to the funny looking boy standing there dripping wet. He turns back towards Freeze. And yells, "And as regards to his name, it's Benjamin." Freeze flips JJ off while he keeps walking away. JJ looks at the crowd and says, "You hear that." "His name is Benjamin." Someone in the crowd begins to whisper, "Benjamin." JJ pauses. Then yells, "That's right, Benjamin." JJ adds. "And for now on you got a problem with Benjamin you got a problem with me." A few people in the crowd whisper, "Benjamin." "Man get out of here it's nothing here to see." JJ yells. The crowd begins to disperse.

JJ turns to Benjamin who is standing there shivering and dripping wet. "C'mon Benjamin," JJ says. "Let's get you dry." He takes Benjamin to the men's bathroom. JJ led Benjamin to one of the toilet stalls.

"Go in there and take all your clothes off and hand them over the door." He tells Benjamin. "OK," Benjamin says in his child-like voice. Benjamin does as he is instructed. JJ stood at the hand dryer for about 15 minutes drying Benjamin's clothes. Then he hands the clothes back over the stall. "Get dressed and come out." He tells Benjamin. Benjamin opens the stall door. He has his shoes on the wrong feet.

"Man," JJ says. "Zip up your pants and button your shirt right." "I mean who wears button ups nowadays anyway and straighten your collar and put your shoes on the right feet." "Here sit down let me help you." JJ says. As Benjamin sits on the commode JJ chuckles to himself. He reminds himself of his mother when she is fussing. "Runs in the family." He says under his breath.

"There, look sharp as a tack, bruh." JJ says as he puts his fist out to give Benjamin a fist bump. Benjamin covers up as if he is going to be hit.

"No, Benji baby boy." JJ says as he pulls Benjamin out of the stoop position he has gone into. "Fist bump." He takes his fist and bumps it together with Benjamin's. Benjamin smiles "We friends," Benjamin says. JJ becomes enraged and grabs Benji by the collar. "Don't ever do that." "We are not friends." "You understand!" JJ yells. "Ok," Benjamin says with a quiver in his timid voice.

JJ relaxes and puts his arm around Benjamin. "I'm sorry Benjamin." JJ says. "I just got a reputation to uphold." "You understand don't you." JJ tells Benjamin. "Ok," Benjamin replies. "C'mon playa let's get to class." JJ walks Benjamin to his class then goes to his own class.

CHAPTER 6

BENJI GETS A NEW NAME

The next day JJ is running to his music class. He reaches the entrance just before the bell rings. Ms. Taylor, a thin older Black lady is standing at the door. Thin and pretty for her age. Only the gray hairs around the crown of her perm told off on her age. "Hold it young man," she says in her sweet smooth voice. "You need to go to the office." She tells him. "But Ms. Taylor." JJ pleads. "I made it before the bell rang," he informs her. "I know you did sweetie," she says to him. "But Mr. Johnson wants to see you." "Oh yes ma'am," he says. "What now," JJ says to himself as he walks to the office. "Looks like I'm going to spend the whole school year in the office." He mumbles to himself.

JJ is greeted by Ms. Summers at the office door. She tells him," Mr. Johnson is waiting on you." JJ steps in the office. He is greeted by Mr. Johnson and coach Smith, a short muscular Black guy who stood about 5'6" with a clean-shaven head and a full mustache and beard and a short man's complex. A miniature Mr. T. "Come on in, Mr. Jenkins. "You know coach Smith don't you?" Mr. Johnson says. "Yes sir," JJ responds as he puts his right hand out to shake the coach's hand. The coach just stares at JJ sternly with his arms folded.

JJ slowly withdraws his hand and has a seat. "Oh boy." JJ thought to himself. "What did I do now?" He ponders. "Let's get to the point, son." Mr. Johnson says. The other day there was an incident with this Swisher kid." Mr. Johnson starts to say. "But sir, I tried to help him out," a defensive JJ interrupts emphatically jumping up from his seat. "I know you did son." "Please don't interrupt me," Mr. Johnson says as sternly as he could in his soft-spoken voice. "Sorry sir," JJ says as he sits back in his seat. "What I was saying, Mr. Jenkins before you interrupted me is, I have talked to coach Smith." "He tells me you are an integral part of both the basketball team and the football team." Both Mr. Johnson and JJ look toward coach Smith. He nods once with an expressionless look on his face. Mr. Johnson adds, "So therefore I am going to lift your 2-games suspension for football." A smile comes to JJ's face, but it instantly disappears when he sees the expression of discontent on Coach Smith's face. "Thank you, sir," JJ hesitantly says to Mr. Johnson.

"One catch though, son." Mr. Johnson adds. "Uh oh." JJ thinks. "Here we go." Detention after school or trash pickup." JJ thinks as the consequences roll through his mind. "Mr. Jenkins have you thought of what you are going to do for your Senior project?" Mr. Johnson asks JJ. "Senior project," JJ thinks in his head. "I am a jock." JJ says. "Something in sports probably." He thought. "I mean it's not due till May 3." "I have plenty of time to think of something, sir." JJ says. "Well Mr. Jenkins work on it no more." "I have talked to Miss Taylor your homeroom teacher." Mr. Johnson says. "And, Mr. Smith and I have come up with the perfect class project for you."

"You have," JJ inquires as he looks at Mr. Smith. For the first time Mr. Smith smiles. Not that happy smile but, a devious smile. He gives JJ the thumbs up "aok" sign and winks his right eye. "Yes son. Mr. Jenkins, we have decided you will be a perfect mentor for Mr. Swisher." Mr. Johnson says. A shocked look comes on JJs face. He looks at Mr. Smith. Mr. Smith just smiles at him nodding in affirmation.

JJ takes a big gulp and answers, "But sir, I have never been a mentor." JJ says. "Well, Mr. Jenkins, it's about time you learned." "Don't you think so Mr. Smith," Mr. Johnson asks Mr. Smith. Mr. Smith remains silent; he just nods his head in agreement. "Yes sir," a disappointed JJ says as he sinks down in his seat. "I tell you what," Mr. Johnson adds. "I am going to take your suspension off your record. He takes some papers out of his desk and tears them up. "How is that." "Like it never happened," he says. "Thank you, sir," JJ replies dryly.

"Well, that will be all you may be dismissed." "Thank you, Mr. Jenkins." "Thank you, Mr. Smith." Mr. Johnson says. The two of them exit the office together. JJ turns to Mr. Smith and puts his hand out to shake Mr. Smith's hand. "Thank you again, sir." JJ tells Mr. Smith. Mr. Smith looks at JJ then firmly grabs his hand and says, "No boy." "Thank you," as he squeezes JJ's hand. "Thanks to you," he says in his gruff deep voice. "I got a retardo in my locker room as towel boy." JJ begins to grimace in pain from the tight hold Mr. Smith has on his hand. "Now you listen to me boy." "It is your responsibility to keep that retardo kid out of my hair, you understand?" Mr. Smith says. "Mr. Smith." an anguished JJ pleads wincing in pain. "This is my shooting hand you are squeezing." Mr. Smith eases up on his grip on JJ's hand and slowly turns and walks away.

JJ shakes the sting of the handshake off and goes to his class. Sitting in the front of class is Benjamin. JJ puts a book to the side of his face and tries to slip to the back of the class. "Mr. Jenkins." He hears Ms. Taylor call his name. "Yes, ma'am," he answers. "We have reserved a special seat up front for you." "My instructions are that you want to sit with Mr. Swisher," she tells him. The class erupts in laughter. JJ gets up in disgust and slowly goes to the front of the class to sit next to Benjamin. Time goes by slowly. JJ thought it was the longest class he ever had. Next class was math. And each class that JJ went to each teacher had instructions that JJ sit next to Benjamin.

"Humiliating," JJ thinks. Last class was gym class. Freeze was in the class with JJ. JJ walks up to Freeze. Freeze turns away from JJ and talks to another friend of theirs, Big Mo. "Can you tell him," Freeze says to Big Mo. "That I'm not speaking to him." JJ turns around, "That's fine with me," JJ says as he walks away from Freeze. "Tell JJ maybe his new friend could be his basketball partner." Freeze says. JJ says, "We don't need other people to talk for us, we can stop talking to each other all together." JJ tells Freeze. Freeze says to Big Mo, "Tell him I don't need a partner." "He could be replaced by anybody." JJ says. "Oh, yeah." Freeze says. "Yeah." JJ says. Big Mo says, "Look you two are trippin' if you think I am going to be the go-between between the two of you."

The two stood there in each other's faces. While Benjamin and Big Mo shot basketballs. Benjamin walks out on the court while Big Mo was shooting basketballs. Big Mo began to pass the ball to Benjamin. JJ continues to argue with Freeze. Benjamin shot a shot from the free-throw. He makes it. Benjamin takes another pass from Big Mo. Benjamin takes a shot from the top of the key. He makes it. Big Mo passes the ball back to Benjamin. Big Mo tries to get JJ and Freeze attention.

"Look guys," Big Mo calls out again. JJ and Freeze continue to argue. Big Mo tries to get their attention. "Look guys!" Big Mo calls out to JJ and Freeze. They continue to argue. Big Mo takes his shoe off and throws it at them. He yells, "Look over here." He finally gets the two to stop arguing with each other for enough time to get their attention.

Big Mo throws the ball to Benjamin. Benjamin shoots the ball from the right corner. He makes it. He passes the ball to Benjamin again. Benjamin shoots the ball from the right corner again. He makes it. He passes the ball back to Benjamin. Benjamin makes the basket from the left corner. He passes the ball back to Benjamin. Benjamin makes it from the half court.

"Well look at that." Freeze says. "The little munchkin can shoot ball," Freeze says rubbing Benjamin's head. "Leave him alone," JJ says. "Why are you always bullying people?" JJ says. "He's not messing with anybody."

"Well ok mother duck." Freeze says. "Let me leave you alone with your little duckling." Freeze says as he storms off the court out of the gym. JJ asks Big Mo for the ball. He begins passing the ball to Benjamin. Benjamin makes 12 shots in a row. "Wow who would have thought?" JJ says. "Hey, Big Mo, this is our secret weapon." "Wait till we tell coach." "Matter fact, I've got a new name for him." "Instead of Benjamin." JJ says.

"Oh yeah." Big Mo says. "What's his new name?" Big Mo asks. JJ says, "From now on Benjamin, you will be known as Swish." "Do you like that Benjamin?" JJ asks Benjamin. Benjamin shakes his head with a big grin. "Ok, Swish it is." JJ says.

Big Mo comes over to JJ. "OK, if you gonna do this we gotta do it right." Big Mo says. JJ says, "OK, come over here Swish." JJ is standing up on one of the bleachers. He is standing over Swish. Big Mo comes and stands next to them with his hand in position to give a salute. JJ begins the cantation. "All right, hear ye, hear ye we officially dub thee Benjamin A Swisher to be hereby known as Swish." Big Mo salutes and makes the sound of a trumpet.

Then Big Mo asks, "What's the "A" stand for?" JJ says, "I don't know." "I don't know if he even has a middle name." "I just added that in there because it sounds more official." JJ explains. "Oh." Big Mo says. "I guess his name with a middle initial does sound more official." Big Mo says.

The bell rings and the three boys run off to their next class.

CHAPTER 7

THE FIELD TRIP

The next day was the first big field trip of the year. It was time to go to the concert to listen to some boring music, but they didn't mind. They would do anything to get out of class. The big blue bus came, and the kids rushed to get on the bus. Freeze and JJ get on the bus but unlike other times they sit separately. Swish gets on the bus, but no one will let him sit next to them. Finally, the music teacher, Miss Taylor, gets on the bus. She looks around the bus and leads Swish to sit next to JJ. The kids begin to laugh.

"Man on the bus, too?" JJ complains. "Can't I get a break sometime?" JJ pleads. "He is your responsibility." Miss Taylor says. Everybody laughs, but nobody laughs harder than Freeze. "Yeah babysitter." Freeze teases JJ. JJ just rolls his eyes and sits down disgustedly. "Hi JJ," says Swish waving his hand. "Look," JJ says to Swish, "Don't say nothing to me." JJ warns Swish. "Ok." Swish says sadly and sinks down in his seat.

The bus arrives at the amphitheater. The music is playing already. They get off the bus and Miss Taylor gets them all in one line. "Ok boys this way and girls that way", she says. "JJ hold Mr. Swisher's hand." Miss Taylor says. The kids begin to laugh. Patricia Torres begins to make funny baby noises. "Don't let the baby get away," she says as she makes baby faces.

"Oh, that's so sweet," Freeze says as he taunts JJ. Reluctantly, JJ holds Swish's hand as they go into the auditorium. The music begins to play. Sure enough as the slow music plays JJ gets sleepy. He dozes off. As he sleeps, he can hear the serene music playing in the background. And he falls asleep.

He is awakened by the voice of Miss Taylor calling his name. "Wake up JJ," she whispers. "It's time to go." As Miss Taylor gets the group together and the boys and girls begin to line up, they are still listening to the piano being played in the background as they get ready to depart the amphitheater. Miss Taylor gets a count of the kids. She keeps coming up one short.

"Who is missing," she says to the group. Everybody looks around. Finally, someone says, "Where is Benjamin?" "Where is Mr. Jenkins?" Miss Taylor asks. Everybody looks at JJ. "Where is Benjamin," everybody says. JJ looks puzzled and puts his arms up as if to say, "I don't know."

"Ooh, you in trouble now." Freeze says to JJ. "You done let retardo monster loose in the city." Freeze says with his hand in JJs face. JJ swipes at Freeze's hand but Freeze moves his hand in time that JJ misses.

Everyone starts looking for Swish now. The music in the background appears to get louder. JJ is frantically looking all over for Swish. He walks up upon one of the girls in the class who was standing in the entrance looking at what was going on in the auditorium. She was looking up on stage. She had a starry glaze in her eyes. He saw it was Maria.

He walks up to her. She was so transfixed she didn't notice him walk up. "Maria," JJ calls her name. She says nothing. She just keeps staring ahead transfixed, staring at the stage. "Maria," he calls her name again. This time he snaps his fingers in front of her face. She jumps like she is coming out of a trance. "Oh hi, JJ," she says. "Maria we're looking for Swish." "Have you seen him?" JJ asks. She slowly shakes her head up and down to indicate, "yes".

"You have, where is he?" JJ asks. She looks at JJ bewildered. Then she slowly points to the stage. JJ looks at the stage. He squints through the bright stage lights to see who is on stage. On stage is Swish playing classical music on the piano. Now JJ is transfixed looking at Swish on stage. He is on the piano.

One by one everyone in the class comes to see what Maria and JJ are looking at. Each person including Miss Taylor is speechless when they see Swish up there playing classical music. The last person to come and watch was Freeze.

"Well, did we find retardo," he jokingly says. "Shush," everybody tells Freeze. Then Freeze sees everyone looking forward towards the stage. He looks towards the stage. He steps forward to get a better look. Freeze sees Swish on the piano playing Tchaikovsky, then Mozart, then Beethoven, then Bach. Freeze is speechless. All of a sudden everyone stops what they're doing and they're looking in amazement at this young man playing on the piano. Everyone who is looking is awestruck and amazed. Who would've thought that such an odd boy would be playing the piano? Even the members of the orchestra have stopped to watch Swish. Nobody moved. Even Miss Taylor stands in amazement. Everyone in the auditorium just stood there starstruck, not knowing what to say.

Finally, Swish plays the last note. He closes the piano, gets up and takes a bow and walks down off the stage. Everyone just stares at him as they make a path for him to walk through the gathering that has stopped to watch him. The gathering of students follows him to the bus. No one says a word. Swish just walks to the back of the bus and lays down on the backseat. He curls up and goes to sleep.

Everybody got on the bus without saying a word. All eyes were on Swish. The silence was deafening. Everyone sat on the bus quietly, even Miss Taylor. Even Freeze, the class clown, even he was quiet and not joking around as he usually is. When Freeze gets on the bus, he sees Swish lying down on the back of the bus. Freeze starts to go towards the back of the bus where Swish was lying. JJ gets up to stop him, thinking he is going to do something detrimental to Swish. Big Mo stops JJ and pushes JJ back down in his seat.

"Relax" Big Mo says. "It's cool." Big Mo tells JJ. "Just watch." Big Mo tells JJ. Freeze walks back to the seat Swish was lying on. Then Freeze takes his jacket off and covers Swish with it. Freeze walks back to his seat. Then he looks back at Swish. "He is special." Freeze says, as he looks back at Swish. "Yeah, he is special". Freeze repeats. "We have to take care of him." On the entire trip back on the bus there was silence.

When the bus gets back to the school Miss Taylor asks to speak to JJ. "Yes, Miss Taylor." JJ says. Miss Taylor reminds JJ that she had assigned Swish to him. And that his failure in this assignment would reflect on his semester grade. When JJ gets home his mother asks how his field trip went. He tells her, "Okay, I guess."

He tells her about what happened with Swish. "Wow", JJ's mother says. "That's amazing." There was a moment of silence.

Then he tells her, "Ma, I am burnt out." She asks him, "Why, baby?" He tells her, "Ma it is a hard task keeping up with Swish." "Well pray about it, baby," she tells him. Another moment of silence.

Then JJ says, "Mom every time I mention a problem you say pray about it." "But why would God curse me to put me in this situation?" He asks his mother. "Well baby, you saw what Swish did today?" She asks him. "Yeah, Ma." He answers her. "I did." She then asks, "Would you say Swish is special?" JJ thinks about it. "Yes ma'am, I would say he is special," JJ responds. "Well son, you are asking the wrong question." His mother tells him.

"What do you mean, Ma?" He asks her. His mother says, "If Swish is special and God has chosen you as his guardian, you should be asking God, "What is so special about you that God saw fit to put you in charge of His special treasure like Swish?" "That out of all the people in the world he put this responsibility on you." She went on to say, "That's not a curse, son." "That's an honor." "God doesn't just choose anybody to do his work, son."

JJ thinks about what his mother said. "You mean God has appointed me as Swish's guardian angel," JJ asks. "Well son," his mother says. "I wouldn't quite say angel." "You're not quite an angel yet and I'm not in a rush for you to become one." She tells him. "But you are his appointed guardian here on earth." His mother says.

A moment of silence as JJ thinks about this. Then JJ asks, "Why me, Ma?" JJ asks his mother. His mother shakes her head. "Wrong question again, son," she tells him. "The question is why not you?" "You're thoughtful, you're smart, you're kind-." JJ chimes in, "I'm good looking." They both laugh. Then a moment of silence.

"You know, Ma, I never looked at it that way." "Thanks, Ma." JJ says. "You are welcome, son." She replies. "Why are you old people so smart?" JJ asks her, "Hey." She responds as she corrects him. "Experienced not old." She tells him. They both laugh.

"Ma," JJ says, "I'm going to be the best guardian for God ever." He says. "I know you are, baby." His mother says. "Ma" JJ says, "Yes, son." She replies. "Yo lil Pookie love ya." He tells her. "Love you more baby." His mother replies.

CHAPTER 8

THE LOWER BOTTOMS

After the school field trip JJ felt an obligation to kind of watch over Swish. He starts spending more and more time with Swish. On this day JJ and Swish were out in the park playing on the basketball court. Freeze comes down to the basketball courts. He sees Swish and JJ playing basketball. He watches them for about five minutes shooting the ball. JJ starts feeding Swish the ball. Swish is shooting the ball. JJ stands there watching Swish shoot from all over the court, making most of his shots. Freeze stops shooting and watches Swish shoot the ball making it from all over the court. Freeze goes to stand next to JJ. JJ rolls his eyes and turns away from Freeze.

The two haven't spoken since they blew up against each other. They stand next to each other watching Swish shoot the ball from all over the court, mostly making it. Finally Freeze says "Lil retar"— he catches himself. Then he says, "I mean the lil fella can really shoot can't he." JJ says nothing. He just nods his head.

They stand there silent for a few minutes. Then Freeze says, "Okay this is killin' me." He turns towards JJ and says,

"I'm sorry." "I was wrong." Freeze stoops to his knees with his hands clasped in prayer position. "Please, please forgive me." He asks JJ. JJ turns towards Freeze. He looks down at him on his knees. "Get up from there," he tells Freeze. "You look ridiculous." He holds his hand out to help Freeze up. JJ pulls Freeze to his feet and gives him a hug. "It's all good." JJ says. Both stand there and watch Swish shoot the ball. "Man, that little guy really can shoot," Freeze says. "Yeah," JJ says. "He is a little pistol Pete." The two watch him for a few more minutes.

"Where did he learn to shoot like that?" Freeze asks. "I don't know?" JJ responds. "Why don't you ask him?" Freeze addresses Swish. "Hey, little man." Then Freeze looks at JJ. "It's Okay if I call him little man, right?" JJ nods. Freeze says, "Lil man." Swish stops shooting the ball. "Where did you learn to shoot like that?" Freeze asks. "Watching TV." Swish says. "Watching TV." Freeze repeats what Swish says.

Then Freeze asks JJ. "Where did he learn to play the piano like that?" JJ says nothing; he just cuts his eyes towards Swish. "Oh yeah." Freeze says. "Hey bro, where did you learn to play the piano like that?"

"Watching TV." Swish answers. "Watching TV." "Imagine that." Freeze says. "Geez, I ought to be a genius as much TV as I watch." Freeze says. "Watching girls on TV don't count." JJ says. They both laugh.

As they stand there Slim and Big Baby and a friend of theirs come and play basketball on the other court. Freeze says, "Look what the cat drug in here?" Freeze says as he kept looking down at the other the court giving Slim a dirty look. Slim only smiles.

"Relax now, please." JJ says to Freeze, "We're not looking for no trouble today." JJ tells Freeze. Then Freeze gets an idea. He whispers in JJ's ear. Then he goes down to the other end of the court. "How's bout a little 3 on 3 fellas?" He says shaking Big Baby's hand but looking at Slim.

"I'm down," Slim says. "Put your money where your mouth is." Slim tells Freeze. Slim brings out $200 in $20 bills. "$200 says we win." Freeze says, "You got it." Slim says. "Put up or shut up." Freeze says as he walks over to JJ. JJ whispers in Freeze's ear. "Man we don't have no $200," JJ tells Freeze. "Relax man." Freeze tells JJ. "I got this." "$200 it is."

Slim puts ten $20 bills down on the ground. "One problem?" Slim says. "Who's your third person?" Slim asks. Freeze looks around as if he's looking for someone. Then he looks over at Swish. At this time, they stood Swish at the far end of the park away from them. "We will take that guy over there." Freeze says pointing to Swish. "Huh?" Slim says. "Yeah, I choose that guy standing over there." Freeze says.

Slim looks over at Swish. "You mean that weirdo looking dude over there?" "Man, you might as well give me $200." Slim says to Freeze looking over at Swish. Slim and Big Baby and their friend face off with JJ, Freeze, and Swish.

"We will be Skins this time." Slim says. Slim and Big Baby and their friend take their shirts off. The game was no match. Freeze and JJ mostly passed the ball to Swish. Swish makes it every time he shoots. Final score JJ's team 24, Slim's team 12. Freeze and JJ go to the middle of the court and give each other a high five.

Slim goes down and picks up the money that Freeze had put on the court. "Hey, this ain't no $200," he says. "This is a couple of $20s and some ones." Freeze walks to Slim and snatches the money out of his hand. Slim and Freeze are standing toe to toe now. Slim is now saying, "How do we know that you would've been good on our bet if we had won the game." Slim says. "Well," Freeze says, "You don't want none of this asshole." JJ and Big Baby run and get between them.

JJ says, "Slim this is me, JJ." "You know if you had won, I'd been good for it." Slim looks at JJ. Then he steps back. "Man, you lucky I got mad love for yo' potna." Slim says to Freeze. Freeze goes to pick up the rest of the money. "It's $200 now," Freeze says laughing as he counts the money in front of Slim's face. "OK." Slim says, "You got me." "All is fair in the game." "No holds barred." Slim says. "Yeah, step off asshole," Freeze tells Slim as he hands Slim a $20 bill. "Don't go away mad," Freeze says. "Just go away." Slim throws the $20 bill on the ground. He begins to walk off. Then he turns around and goes back to get the bill off the ground. "You owe me this." Slim says as he picks the bill up and walks off.

"See ya." Freeze says. "Wouldn't wanna be ya." Freeze says counting the money and laughing. In the meantime, JJ is shaking hands with Big Baby and the other friend of Slim's. "Nice game," they say as they congratulate JJ and walk off.

Freeze stands there counting the money in front of them as they walk off shaking their heads. JJ walks over to Freeze. "You need to chill out Freeze," JJ says. "Must you always gloat after we win?" JJ says to Freeze. Sorry I can't help it. "It's in my blood," Freeze says. "My father was a playa therefore I am a playa." Freeze says.

"Yeah, I thought you said you never met your father?" JJ says." "Nope never met the man." Freeze says. "If you never met the man, JJ asks. "How do you know he was a player?" Inquires JJ. Freeze says, "It's obvious, I got so much playa in me he had to be a playa," Freeze informs him.

"Well put this in your blood playa folks." JJ says. "Don't ever pull no shit like that again with me again." He tells Freeze. "Ooh." Freeze says. "I never heard you cuss." Freeze tells JJ. "Well hear me straight." JJ tells Freeze. "The only asshole here today was you." "I don't play games like that." "I play on the up and up." JJ says. "All right." Freeze says, "Sorry won't do it no mo'." "Ok," Freeze says. "But I'm telling Miss Jenkins you was cussing." Freeze says. "That's fair enough." JJ says. "And I'm telling Emma Jones you're dating Sarah Smith, too." JJ says. "Dang." Freeze says. "You ain't gotta get all vicious with it and everything." "OK truce." Freeze says. "Yeah, that's what I thought," JJ says.

They do the pinky handshake.

"Anyway, my mother would understand." JJ says. "Dealing with you will make the Pope curse." JJ tells Freeze.

"How did you learn to blackmail people so well?" Freeze asks JJ. "Learned from the best," JJ says. "You." He tells Freeze. "Dang JJ," Freeze says. "You make it seem like I'm scandalous or something." JJ just looks at him and nods his head.

"OK." JJ says, "Enough small talk." "Give me my money." Freeze gives JJ $100. JJ looks at the $100 then he looks at Swish. "What about Swish?" JJ says. "He deserves something." JJ tells Freeze. "Aw man." Freeze says. "We gotta split it three ways?" Freeze complains. "Lil man don't even know what to do with money." Freeze complains. JJ just looks at Freeze with a stern look. "OK, OK, man." "Don't look at me like that." "We will split it three ways." Freeze says. "But since we got $200 we might as well make some big money." "Let's go to DeFremery Park and play the big boys for some real money." Freeze encourages them. "What you mean to the lower bottoms?" JJ says. "I don't know." JJ says to Freeze. "Dead man's park." "Man those homies are serious about their scrilla over there." "Besides Ma doesn't want me over on that side of town." "It's too much trouble to get into." JJ says to Freeze.

Freeze says to JJ, "Stop being such a wus." "You gonna be a mama's boy all your life?" "Baby boy get some balls." "Let's have some adventure for a change." He tells JJ. "Live on the edge." "Look at all the money we can make." Freeze says. JJ thinks about it.

"OK," JJ says. "Let's go for it. "Come on, Swish." JJ says. The three set out towards the other side of town. The rough side of town. Three of them arrive at DeFremery Park. On the basketball court there are big hairy men with tattoos. Rough looking guys playing basketball. Look like the penitentiary courtyard. Freeze walks up to a guy in all black. "What you want youngsta?" The man asks Freeze. "I want to sign my team up," says. The man looks Freeze up and down. The man is wearing dark sunglasses with a toothpick in his mouth. "It's $100 a team per game." The man says. "Winner take half the pot of those who are betting." The man says. The man looks at Freeze and says, "Looka here youngsta." "We real about our cheddar around here, ya dig?" "So, no shenanigans." The man tells Freeze. Freeze gives the man a thumbs up. The man goes on to say, "Another thing youngsta." "Ain't no choir boys around here." "There is a rough group that hangs out around here." "I'm not responsible for your safety." He says showing Freeze that he is packing heat by lifting up his shirt and showing his piece he wears on his hip. Freeze just nods and gives the man $100. They play the first game, and they win the first game. "Look at there," Freeze says. "See now we got $300 to split." "Like taking candy from a baby." He tells JJ. JJ looks around at the crowd. "More like taking a banana from a gorilla." JJ says. They play the next game and win the next game. They play three more games. Now they have $900 dollars to split between the three of them.

Now was time for the last game. "Winner takes the whole pot." The man in black announces. $2500 If they won this added to the $900 they had won already they would have $1100 plus apiece. "See." Freeze says. "We win this we get $3400 to split." "That's some real scratch."

Right now, there is a break in the action. Freeze goes to the restroom. He steps into one of the stalls and closes the doors. Some other guys come in the bathroom while he's in there. He hears their conversation. Two thugs.

"Who are those young punks come in here winning everything?" One of them says. "I don't know?" Says the other guy that came into the bathroom. "Yeah, they better not win this last final game." The guy says. "Yeah, what you gonna do if they do?" The other guy says. "I'm gonna strip them suckas," he says. "I feel ya." "I'm down wit' it." "Give me a piece of this action." "I'm gonna hit this lick wit 'ya." The other guy says.

Freeze is listening to these guys' conversation as the two slap their hands and snap their fingers. "If they win, it's time to hit a lick." The first guy says. Freeze hears this conversation. He waits till the two guys have left out the bathroom and goes back to JJ.

"Looka' here." Freeze says to JJ. "We gotta problem." Freeze says. He tells JJ of the plot. "Man." JJ says. "I knew we should not have come over here." JJ complains to Freeze. "Don't worry," Freeze says. "I gotta plan." Freeze assures JJ. "Well, I hope this plan involves getting me outta here in one piece." JJ says. "Relax JJ." "I got this." Freeze says. He whispers into JJs ear.

The last game starts. Just as in previous games, Freeze team is winning. They only need one shot to win. Freeze stands outside the court ready to pass the ball in. Freeze passes the ball into JJ. JJ passes the ball to Swish. Swish shoots the ball and makes it for the final score. As soon as the ball goes into the hoop JJ runs and grabs Swish by the hand and takes off running out of the park and doesn't look back.

After running several blocks away from the park JJ stops to catch his breath. He waits for Freeze. He is waiting for more than two hours before finally Freeze runs up to him out of breath with the money in his hands.

"Hey." JJ says. "What took you so long?" "I thought you had fodangled us." JJ says laughing. Freeze hands the money to JJ then falls on the ground. JJ notices blood on the back of Freeze's shirt. "Freeze!" JJ yells. "Get up Freeze!" JJ yells again. JJ helps Freeze to his feet. There is a clinic across the street. JJ and Swish walk Freeze over to the clinic.

JJ sits Freeze in a seat when they get in the clinic.. "We're gonna get you help, potna." JJ tells Freeze. "Hang in there." JJ says. He walks up to a lady wearing white at the counter.

"My friend," JJ tells the lady. "He needs help." "Does your friend have insurance?" The lady asks. "Yes, no, I don't know?" He needs help lady, he's hurt." JJ tells the lady. She gives him some forms to fill out. "Fill these forms," she says. "Lady, he needs help now!" JJ screams.

One of the doctors overhears JJ. He walks over. "Can I help you, young man?" The doctor asks JJ. "Yes, sir." A frantic JJ says. "My friend, he's been injured." "He needs help." JJ tells the doctor almost hyperventilating. The doctor stands there staring at JJ. "Here, we have $3400." JJ says as he hands the doctor the winning pot.

The doctor hands the money back to JJ. "That won't be necessary." The doctor says. "Put your money in your pocket." "Nurse, get some interns over here and get this young man on a gurney." The doctor says. They roll Freeze on a gurney into the emergency room.

The next day JJ goes back to the hospital. He goes to the room where Freeze is. Freeze is laying on his left side. "Hey man." JJ yells out to Freeze. "You know there easier ways of getting days off from school." JJ tells Freeze. Freeze puts a big grin on his face. "I know." Freeze says. "But those ways are too boring." Freeze tells JJ. JJ sits on the side of Freeze's bed and they both laugh.

They sit quietly for a minute, then JJ says, "Why did you do that?" Freeze asks, "Why did I do what?" Freeze responds. "Why did you risk yourself for me and Swish?" JJ asks. "I mean, I don't know I guess I felt responsible for you two." Freeze says. "I didn't want anything to happen to Swish and I definitely didn't want to have to go back to your mother to have to tell your mother that you got injured because of me." Freeze says. "I'd rather face World War Three." "Anyway it was just a flesh wound." Freeze says. "A flesh wound?" JJ says. "8 stitches." JJ says. "You could run a flatbed truck through it." JJ says. "Doc says it was 2 inches away from your kidney." JJ says. "Well anyway next time this happens we are all in this together." He assures Freeze.

"Exactly." A voice comes from outside the door. "We are all in this together." Freeze and JJ look up. In the door walk in Slim and Big Baby and two other guys. "What's up fellas." Freeze says. Big Baby and Slim walk over and shake Freeze's hand and give him a little hug. "Yeah, you guys foolish going on the other side of town by yourselves." "Next time you decide to do a fool thing like that." Slim says. "Holla at yo boy." Slim says. "Word up." Freeze says. "You guys stay up." Slim says. "We gotta go down the hallway and see Big Baby's Grammy." They say goodbye to each other.

"Wow." Freeze says. "Didn't know Slim cared." "Yeah." JJ says. "Slim is cool people." "For an asshole." They both say simultaneously. They both laugh.

"Hey how long are you gonna be in this hospital?" JJ asks Freeze. "Doctor says I should be outta here by tomorrow." Freeze says. "OK, you know we still gotta get ready for football season." JJ says to Freeze. Freeze gives JJ a thumbs up. "Oh I'm ready." Freeze says. "Bring it on." JJ and Freeze embrace and JJ leaves.

CHAPTER 9

FOOTBALL SEASON

It was the third week of September. It was time for the football season to start. JJ and Freeze were on the practice field. As usual Swish was there as their sidekick. Coach Ferrero the football coach was easier going than Coach Smith. He even got Swish a uniform for the team. JJ was kind of getting used to Swish hanging around. Matter fact the whole team was fond of him. He was like the team mascot. Because of JJ his superstar quarterback coach put Swish on the roster. Unlike basketball the school team had never been competitive in baseball and football. In the three years JJ had been quarterback and Freeze had been the wide receiver. The team had won only four games out of 30.

So, there was no big expectation in the football season. The first game they played they played against Hogan High. Hogan High was probably the only team sorrier than them. As expected they beat Hogan High 12 nothing in a low scoring game.

The next team they played was Lakeside High. Lakeside was one of the teams predicted to win the playoffs. In the best game JJ and Freeze have played in their high school career they pull it off and upset Lakeside High. Winning a close game 35 to 32.

The next game was even closer against a more potent opponent. The Dogwood Dragons. They were 12-point underdogs to Dogwood but ended up winning the game 21 to 20.

For the first time in the four years that JJ and Freeze had been at AT High the team had a chance to have an undefeated season. The next game was against Bush High. Again they were underdogs. But AT ended up winning a squeaker 27 to 25.

Next, on the schedule was Danville. If they beat Danville, they would go to the divisional championship game against Scottsdale. The game against Danville was a ferocious game. The score went back-and-forth. But in the end AT High won on a last second field goal. For the first time JJ and Freeze had led their team to the divisional championship game.

The next opponent they played was powerful Scottsdale. In the four years that JJ and Freeze were at AT High School Scottsdale had won three titles and it only lost one game and that was to Douglas Dogwood. The last time they played Scottsdale they lost to Scottsdale 35 to 0.

Now it's time for the playoffs. Scottsdale being undefeated again stormed into the playoffs easily. Winning by an average of outscoring their opponents by 30 points a game. AT High was to play Scottsdale for the regional championship. It was a week before the championship game. The team was at practice on the AT football field. The players were throwing the ball around. JJ threw a pass to Freeze. The pass went over Freeze's head. Swish ran to get the ball. Then he started running down field with the ball. He kept running even after the other players tried to stop him. Other players chased him to get the ball. Swish dodged all of them. He was able to dodge everyone trying to stop him till he made it to the end zone. When he got to the end zone, he did a little victory dance.

JJ finally caught up with him. "Swish stop playing and give us the ball," JJ yells as he snatches the ball from Swish. "Sorry," Swish says to JJ. Remembering how sensitive Swish is, JJ puts his arm around him. "It's OK." Swish JJ says. In the meantime, Freeze is just nodding his head looking at Swish.

A week later the team is pumped up about the game they are going to have with Scottsdale for the regional championship. The game starts off disappointing. Scottsdale's scores touchdowns on its first two possessions. At the end of the first quarter the score is 14 to nothing. Scottsdale leading.

It looks like Scottsdale is going to rout AT High again. The Scottsdale High players are already giving each other high fives as if they have already won the game. At the end of the first quarter the AT coach decides to put his best players playing defense and offense. Of those four players JJ and Freeze are two of those players.

At half time it was 14 to nothing in favor of Scottsdale.. The coach of AT had stopped the bleeding in that he stopped Scottsdale from scoring, but AT could not score on Scottsdale's superior defense. At half time the coach gave the team a pep talk.

Coach figured out that if they could keep Scarsdale from scoring, they had a chance to win. The third quarter was scoreless. The beginning of the fourth-quarter begins with Scottsdale waiting to receive the kickoff. The ball was kicked off to Scottsdale. They received it on their 30-yard line. The runner grabs the ball and begins running with it. Just as he was going to be tackled, he pitches the ball back to another Scottsdale runner and this runner runs the ball over 50 yards for a touchdown.

Now the score was 21 to nothing in favor of Scottsdale.. The score seemed insurmountable. As time ticked down Scottsdale fans and team began to celebrate prematurely. They could feel victory in the air. With five minutes to go, Scottsdale had to punt the ball.

Freeze was observing the field. He whispered something to the coach. The coach calls a time out. Freeze had an idea. The coach looks at Freeze. "This better work," coach tells Freeze. "Trust me," coach Freeze says. "I got this." "When it works you can take credit for it;" Freeze says.

Scottsdale goes to punt. This time lined up on the field is Swish in the back field. The ball is punted. Freeze receives the punt. He runs a couple of steps. And throws the ball back to JJ. JJ runs a couple steps and laterals the ball back to Swish. Swish stands there. JJ says "Run!" Swish begins to run.

Scottsdale teammates begin to chase after him. Swish runs the length of the field. "Touchdown!" The man in stripes yells as he raises his hands and Swish crosses the goal line.

Finally AT is on the scoreboard. AT makes its extra point and now the game is 21 to 7. "Now we're cooking with grease," the coach of AT says to his team. Coach Ferrero says, "Defense let's hold 'em." Once again, the AT defense holds the Scottsdale team from scoring. Now there are three minutes remaining in the game. Once again Swish is on the field to receive the ball. Last time they caught Scottsdale off guard. This time the players would be ready for the speedy evasive Swish, or so they thought.

Once again, the ball is kicked off. This time the ball goes straight to Swish. JJ and Freeze are right in front of him to block for him. Swish runs down field with JJ and Freeze blocking for him. They blocked the first two Scottsdale players that tried to tackle Swish. Swish gets away from another player and evades a tackle from a fourth player. Again, Swish out runs the rest of the field. Again, the referee raises his arms, "Touchdown!" The official yells out. Now the AT crowd is ecstatic and the Scottsdale crowd for the first time in four years is nervous. Swish antics have snatched the smell of victory out of the air for Scottsdale. Now the score is 21 to 14.

Problem is there is only a minute left. And AT is down by seven points and kicking off the ball. Their only hope is an on-side kick. The coach for AT lines the team up to do an on sides kick. Both teams lineup ready to fight for the ball. The AT kicker squibble kicks the ball. A free for all happens on the field. There is a battle on the ground for the ball. Players from both teams are piled up on each other. The referee gets over to separate the teams. after separating the pile up JJ comes out the pile with the ball on the Scottsdale 35-yard line. AT side of the field erupts in cheers while the Scottsdale side grumbles.

AT coach calls a timeout. AT huddles up on the sidelines. Again, Swish is lined up on the far-right side. The coach for Scottsdale lines three of his defensive players opposite Swish. JJ takes his position behind the center. The ball is hiked to JJ. JJ steps back like he is going to throw the ball to Swish. Practically the whole Scottsdale Defense gravitates towards Swish. JJ pauses and pulls the ball back. Then he looks towards the end zone where Freeze is standing in the end zone by himself. JJ floats the ball to Freeze. Freeze catches the ball. "Touchdown," the referees yells with his hands in the air: Freeze goes into his touchdown dance. The AT crowd goes wild. The Scottsdale crowd gives out a sigh of disgust. Now the score is Scottsdale 21 to AT 20.

AT coach calls for a timeout. A discussion is held on the sidelines with the team. Again, AT comes out with Swish in the lineup. AT has decided to go for the two-point conversion for the win instead of the tie. The Scottsdale team seems more confused than ever now. Half of the team goes towards Freeze lined up on the left opposite end and the other half goes towards Swish lined up on the right end.

The ball is hiked by the center to JJ. This time JJ fakes throwing the ball to Freeze then laterals the ball to Swish. Swish just stands there. "Run." JJ says. Swish starts running but in the wrong direction. He has 21 other players chasing after him. Freeze is the only one who could outrun him and catch him. Freeze catches him just before he steps over the goal line of the opposite goal.

"The other way, Swish the other way!" Freeze yells. Swish turns around and starts running down the field the other way. Freeze picks off the first defensive player trying to tackle him. Another player comes at Swish. Swish runs 10 yards backwards to evade this player. Two other players are coming at him. Swish runs sideline to sideline to evade them. Now Swish is at the 50-yard line. He picks up a block from JJ.

And he picks up another block from another AT player. He has managed to make it to the 30-yard line of Scottsdale. One more player stands in the way between him and the goal line. The player lunges at Swish. Swish ducks and the Scottsdale player flies over his head. Now Swish out runs everybody behind him and crosses the goal line as time runs out. The referee raises both arms and yells, "Score"! The sound of the starter pistol rings out signaling the end of the game. "Two-point conversion," the referee calls.

The Scottsdale fans become eerily silent whereas the AT fans erupt in cheers and rush the field that is strewn with players from both sides of the field who have collapsed from exhaustion chasing Swish.

Both Freeze and JJ lift Swish on their shoulders and all the AT fans are yelling, "S-W-I-S-H," "S-W-I-S-H," "S-W-I-S-H," "S-W-I-S-H," as they carried Swish off the field with the scoreboard showing Scottsdale 21 and AT 22.

Freeze says up to Swish sitting on his and JJ's shoulders, "Where did you learn how to run a football like that, buddy?" Freeze asks Swish. "Watching TV." Swish responds. "Watching TV." Freeze says. "Figures." JJ says, "We are going to go get some Rocky Road ice cream," JJ tells Swish. "Yay," Swish says as they leave the stadium.

CHAPTER 10

BASKETBALL AND BASEBALL SEASON

September and October went by really fast, so it was time for a high school basketball game in November. JJ was starting shooting guard for the team along with Freeze was the starting point guard and Big Mo the starting center on the team. With the Robinson twins at starting forwards. Guerrero and Dwight White were part of the bench. Since Swish was to follow JJ around they made him the team mascot and water/ towel boy.

Being with the team helped improve Swish's image. Not only had JJ and Freeze appointed themselves as Swish's personal guardians, but people love Swish's childlike carefree personality. That is everybody but Coach Smith.

Coach Smith still resents having to have Swish with the team. He often verbally abuses Swish. Coach Smith calls Swish names like psycho, dumbo, stupid, idiot, but his favorite name for Swish is retardo.

One day Freeze tells JJ, "Coach Smith sure is hard on Swish, isn't he?" JJ looks over at Coach Smith going into a tirade against Swish. "Yeah man." JJ says. "But we can't say anything." JJ says, "And risk being thrown off the team." Freeze looks back at the coach going off on his tirade berating Swish. "I guess." JJ says. "Yeah, I guess you're right." Freeze, says.

The chastisement didn't seem to bother Swish at all. He was the team gofer and seemed to enjoy it. On one occasion in the middle of practice while the coach was giving the boys a pep talk, Swish comes to the coach with a towel. Coach turns red in the face and goes on one of his tirades.

"No, you bungling idiot." Coach yells. "I said my clipboard, not a towel." Coach knocks the towel out of Swish's hand. "You damn fool, get out of here," Coach yells. Tears began to well up in Swish's eyes. "Sorry." Swish says in his timid childlike voice. "Sorry, hell." Coach yells at Swish. "Get the hell out of here." Coach Smith yells as he grabs Swish by the arm and pulls him to the exit. "Sorry," a tearful Swish says again. "Yeah, you sorry all right." "I want your sorry ass out of my gym," Coach says. "Get the hell out of here," He tells Swish while he pushes him out the door and closes the door behind him. "And don't come back." The Coach emphatically says.

"Now where was I?" "Oh, yeah." Coach says. He looks up at the group. He notices Freeze is walking away. "Where are you going, son?" Coach asks Freeze. Freeze says nothing. He just goes to sit in the middle of the court in the circle on the court. Coach asks Freeze again. "What you doing, son?" Coach asks looking at Freeze. "Practice is over, Coach." Freeze answers. "What do you mean practice is over, you been smoking them funny cigarettes or something?" Coach asks Freeze. "We got at least two more hours of practice." The coach says. "Not me Coach," Freeze says. "Not me until you call Swish in here and apologize to him." Freeze says. "What you talking about boy?" Coach fumes. "Apologize to him?" "You want me to apologize to that freak?" Coach says. "When hell freezes over."

Freeze sits in silence. "Fine then." Coach says. "You want to give up your basketball career for that retarded bastard, that's fine with me." "We will play without you." The coach tells Freeze. "Everyone else give me five laps around the court." Coach tells the team.

The team just stands there. "You heard me five laps around the court." The coach says. JJ goes to the center of the court and has a seat with Freeze. One by one the rest of the team follows suit. Coach says, "You guys willing to give up the season for him?" No one says a word. They all sit in silence. The coach stands silently with his arms folded.

Finally, Coach says, "OK, bring the little retard-," Coach catches himself, "I mean get the young man in here." Freeze steps out the gym and brings Swish back in with his arm around Swish's shoulders. Swish is still sobbing. "Calm down Swish." Freeze says. "Coach has something to tell you."

Freeze stands Swish in front of the coach. Coach just stands there. "What?" Coach says as if he was at a loss of words. The rest of the team comes to stand with Freeze and Swish. "Tell him Coach, that you apologize for being mean to him," Freeze says. The coach takes a hard swallow and looks at Swish and says, "I apologize, son, for being mean to you." Then Freeze says "And, tell him Coach that from now on you will not call him anymore names." The coach says, "And I from now on son, will not call you anymore names." Then JJ adds "And from now on Swish is a part of the team and will get a uniform." "Oh, no." Coach says, "That's not going to happen."

The rest of the team goes and sits back in the circle. Coach stands there with his arms folded. "Ok." Coach says, "You are a member of the team and we will get you a uniform." The team stands up and cheers. They all gather around Freeze and Swish celebrating. "Five laps!" Freeze yells out while he and the team lead Swish to his doing his first five laps as an official member of the team. All the players are yelling, "Swish", "Swish," "Swish." "This is a mutiny." Coach says under his breath.

The season always ended with their team and St. Francis going undefeated till the last game of the season. They always ended up playing St. Francis in the regional championship game. For the past three years St. Francis had defeated them in the regional finals. And gone on to win the State championship. Three years in a row. JJ and Freeze and the other senior players felt this was the year that they could beat Saint Francis. The basketball season went as usual.

Amanda Thompkins High (AT High) blew through the competition every year to get to the regional finals only to lose to St. Francis by a couple of points. Last year they lost in a buzzer beater by one point. So, this is what they have been waiting for. Once again here the teams were. St. Francis and AT High.

The referee gave the signal, and the game began. AT High gets off to a good start. After 3 quarters it looks like AT High might win. They were up by 12 points through three quarters. But then disaster strikes. Freeze, their best player, is hobbling on the court. He comes to the sidelines. It appears he has sprained his ankle. "No more basketball for you today." The team trainer says. "Damn!" Freeze says emphatically as he hobbles to the bench. "Now what do we do?" Big Mo says. Freeze takes the grimace of pain off his face and tries to encourage the team by showing a brave face. "We go kick some ass." Freeze says. "Who are we," Freeze says. The team says, "AT High, in a less than enthusiastic tone. "What was that?" Freeze says. "We can do better than that." "Now once again, who are we!" Freeze yells! The team yells, "AT High!" The team yells. "I didn't hear you!" Freeze yells. "Who are we?" The team shouts. "AT High!" Freeze yells, "We ride together!" JJ yells. "We die together!" The whole team yells. "I am my brother's keeper!" They break ranks cheering running onto the court.

AT High was putting up a valiant battle. But without their best player Freeze in the lineup Saint Francis starts cutting into AT High's lead. Only thing Freeze could do was be a cheerleader on the sidelines. With AT Highs best player sidelined Saint Francis players were double and triple teaming AT High's next best player, which was JJ. With twelve seconds to go the St. Francis guard hits a three pointer to put St. Francis up by two points. AT coach calls a timeout.

He starts setting up a play for JJ. Then Freeze remembers how Swish had been shooting the ball from half court. "Hey coach." Freeze gets the coach's attention. "Yeah, son." Coach Smith answers. "Let's use our secret weapon." "Seeing you know with me out they are gonna double team JJ." "Let's make a play with our secret weapon." Freeze says. "And who is our secret weapon?" Coach inquires. Freeze whispers in the coach's ear. "Oh, no." Coach says, "Are you serious?" He asks Freeze. "Trust me on this one, Coach," Freeze says. The coach looks at Freeze for a second, then nods approval. "This better work", the coach tells Freeze.

Freeze tells the coach, "Coach, I got this."

Freeze calls Swish over and explains to Swish and the rest of the team the play. Freeze tells the team to "Break on three, three"," and the team yells, "I am my brother's keeper, as they take their positions on the court. "Remember Swish, stand right here in the far corner and when we pass you the ball, shoot towards the basket." "Understand?" JJ tells Swish. "Ok." Swish replies.

The horn sounds to restart the game and Swish is led to the far-right corner of the half court. The St. Francis side of the auditorium begins laughing and clowning around. "Awe looks like a monkey on the court," someone says. "You guys going out like suckas, putting Special Ed on the court," another Saint Francis fan says. "It's a diversion." The coach from Saint Francis says. "Keep your eyes on that JJ boy." He tells the team.

Big Mo took the ball out. He throws the ball in to one of the Robinson twins, who quickly throws the ball to Guerrero, who quickly throws the ball to JJ. When JJ gets the ball three Saint Francis players converge on him. JJ quickly whips the ball over to Swish with five seconds left. Swish stands there a second holding the ball.

"Shoot the ball", JJ yells to Swish. The AT bench shouts. "Shoot the ball!" The crowd yells, "Shoot the ball," as the clock winds down, 3, 2,1. Swish shoots the ball. Everything seems to be moving in slow motion as the arc of the ball descends down towards the basket.

"Swish," the sound of the ball going through the bottom of the net as the horn to end the game sounds simultaneously. First there was an utter silence at the amazement that a person of Swish's statue had made the basket from half court. Then simultaneously the AT crowd and the AT bench gave out a big roar as they stormed the court, while the Saint Francis team and fans stood there in shock.

The AT fans were yelling, "Swish!" "Swish!" "Swish!" Coach Smith, still in disbelief, was standing there next to the coach of the other team. He was still in shock that they had won. The coach of the other team threw his clipboard to the floor and said, "Beaten by retardo." Coach Smith approaches Saint Francis's coach and says, pointing his finger in the coach's face, "His name is Swish." Then, Coach Smith runs off the court yelling, "Swish!" "Swish!" "Swish!"

Seems like the month of March came around fast. Like basketball and football JJ and Freeze were on the baseball team. Unlike football and basketball, they were benchwarmers on the baseball team. This suited them fine. They weren't really great baseball fans. They were on the team only because it gave them a reason to be out of class.

Still, they brought Swish along and he became the team mascot. Swish really didn't show any special baseball skills like he did in the other two sports other than he was a great water boy and equipment manager. But many thought he was a good luck charm. The baseball team went undefeated while Swish was their mascot.

They ended up the season 30 and zero. And won the Triple Crown. The baseball championship. The basketball championship. And the football championship. The first time ever that AT High had done this in its 80-year history. The school year keeps rolling along. Now the month of May has crept up on them.

CHAPTER 11

THE TALENT SHOW

Freeze and JJ are chilling on a bench in the school Quad. Freeze throws some water out of his water bottle on JJ. The water smacks JJ in the face. JJ stands up blinking. "Oh, it's on now." JJ says, reaching into his backpack getting a bottle of water. The two run through the campus exchanging water tosses. Both of them laughing and running carefree, not paying much attention to the surrounding area. JJ aims a water shot at Freeze. Freeze ducks and the water hits Mr. Johnson in the face. Both of them stopped what they were doing and stood there in shock. JJ takes a napkin out of his bag and hands it to Mr. Johnson. "Well, thank you, sir." Mr. Johnson says. "Quite refreshing, but I did shower this morning." He says in jest.

"Sorry, Mr. Johnson, sir." JJ timidly says. Mr. Johnson says, "Son come to my office." JJ gives a look of dismay. Then Freeze says, "Really sir, I started this." "This is my fault." Freeze assures Mr. Johnson. "Very well," Mr. Johnson says. "I appreciate your honesty." "You come to my office, too." Mr. Johnson says to Freeze. JJ looks at Freeze. Freeze just throws his hands up in the air.

The two young men dismally walk behind Mr. Johnson to his office contemplating what the consequences of their misbehavings were going to be. "Have a seat, young men." Mr. Johnson says as he ushers them into his office. The two young men have a seat. Mr. Johnson pulls out some papers and looks over the papers. Then he looks up at the two young men. "Young men despite your immature appearance I believe you are both brighter than you appear to be right now." Mr. Johnson says. JJ and Freeze are a little confused at where this conversation is going. "So young men I have brought you in here because there's a task that needs to be done." "Do you think the two of you are up to doing a very important task?" Mr. Johnson says as he looks at JJ. "Yes sir Mr. Johnson, anything for you." JJ says. Mr. Johnson looks at Freeze. Freeze nods his head up and down.

"Good young men." Miss Taylor needs some judges for the talent show. Usually, we pick two young men and two young ladies." "So, after school today report to Miss Taylor and she will give you your assignments." Mr. Johnson tells them. "Yes sir, Mr. Johnson." JJ says. "Yes sir," Freeze says to Mr. Johnson.

Mr. Johnson goes back to reading the paper he has in his hand. JJ and Freeze look at each other confused on whether they can leave or not. Finally, JJ gets enough courage to speak. "Excuse me, Mr.

Johnson, sir." JJ asks. Mr. Johnson replies. "Yes, young man." Mr. Johnson responds. "Are we free to leave?" JJ inquires. "Young men, the both of you carry on." Mr. Johnson says.

Both of them get up slowly in shock that they are not in more trouble and slowly they begin to exit the office. Mr. Johnson catches them before they leave. "Oh, one thing young men." Mr. Johnson says. "Yes sir, Mr. Johnson." They both answer. "Please, don't let me catch the two of you clowning around again." Mr. Johnson tells them. "Yes sir, Mr. Johnson." They say in unison.

They both walk out of the office. JJ grabs his heart, "Man, that was close." JJ says. "Last thing I need to do is get in some more trouble." He tells Freeze. "I feel ya' on that." Freeze says. "I thought we were done for." Freeze tells JJ. "Yeah, I just thank God it wasn't Mr. Jackson." Freeze says. "Oh, shutter the thought." JJ says.

"Thanks, my homie." JJ says to Freeze. "Thanks for what?" Freeze replies. "Thanks for not leaving me hanging." JJ answers. "It was nothing." Freeze says. "I learned my lesson from the last time." Freeze adds.

The bell rings for the next class. "Hey, how about White Castle's on me?" JJ tells Freeze. "Sure, after school I'll see ya'." The two embrace and set off on their separate ways to their classes.

The day of the talent show arrives. It was May 7th. The excitement of the anticipation of Summer break was in the air. Especially, for the seniors who, will be graduating this year. The talent show is an annual event sponsored by Ms. Taylor to raise money for school field trips. This was the day the jugglers and singers and want to be rappers came out to display their talents. Not only did JJ and Freeze have to be judges, but they were also responsible for selling tickets to the event. Only seniors could participate in the talent show in that the winning prize was two tickets to the senior prom.

Miss Taylor called JJ and Freeze to her room the day of the talent show. She thanked the both of them for their effort in selling the talent show tickets. She told them that they have sold more tickets than anybody in the time she had been selling talent show tickets.

"Well, you know." Freeze says. "We hustlers." Freeze brags. "And what do you mean by that?" Miss Taylor says in a stern voice with her hands on her hips. "He speaking for himself, Miss Taylor," JJ says. "Way to throw me under the bus." Freeze whispers to JJ. Then Freeze says, "Aw, Miss Taylor." "I mean that in a good way." Freeze says giving Miss Taylor a hug. She pats him on the back. "Get on out of here boy, trying to finesse me." "I am not one of those little girls you be chasing after," she says. "Naw ma'am Miss Taylor." Freeze says. "You way finer than them." Miss Taylor laughs and says, "Boy if you don't get out of here with those dead pickup lines." "OK, Miss Taylor, I'm leaving." Freeze says.

The two of them leave her room. After the boys leave out Miss Taylor takes her mirror and looks at her face in the mirror. As JJ and Freeze are leaving her classroom and walking down the hall, Freeze tells JJ, "She know she wants me." "Who wants you?" JJ asks Freeze. "Miss Taylor, she knows she hot for me." Freeze says. JJ looks at Freeze and shakes his head. "You are a pervert." He tells Freeze. Freeze says, "Yep and I'm gonna be a pervert until I'm a dead vert". He laughs and puts his right hand up to get a high five from JJ. JJ just walks off shaking his head. "Aw JJ," Freeze says running off after him. "You gonna leave me hanging?"

The night of the talent show has arrived. The auditorium is packed with faculty parents and students. There are 12 contestants on the stage. Miss Taylor goes to the microphone and introduces all the contestants along with JJ and Freeze and two other judges.

The first contestant is dressed like a clown. George Peacock. George comes out with his juggling act. He did well all the way to the end when he drops one of the balls. He gets boos. George takes a bow anyway.

The next act was Jeremy Stills, Roger Barnes, and Tyler Martin. They were a rap group that went by the name XYZ. In the middle of the rapping the crowd wasn't too pleased with them. They booed them off the stage.

The next act was Alice Colbert. She did a scene from the play "Gone with the Wind." She got a lukewarm applause. The next few acts rolled by quickly, until they got to the next to the last act. This act was Tonya James.

Tonya sings a rendition of Aretha Franklin's "Respect." She got a rousing ovation after she finished.

Finally, there was the last act. This was Maria Consuelo. Maria was a great singer. She was expected to win the competition. After all she had already appeared at the opera house singing the aria from the opera "Carmen", "The Toreador Song." This time she would sing the aria from the opera, "Evita." "Don't Cry for Me Argentina." She started off the song low key but then began to crescendo as the song continued to the end and she ended the song on a high note. A note so high that you wondered if the glasses were going to break. She got a rousing round of applause.

After the last act Miss Taylor came to the microphone. "We will now tabulate the vote." Miss Taylor says. As they were tabulating the votes there was a buzz in the auditorium of people talking to each other while they anticipated the outcome. Suddenly, everybody gets quiet.

Miss Taylor comes to the microphone. "For the first time," Miss Taylor says. "In this competition, we have a tie between Tonya James and Maria Consuelo." "When we have a tie," Miss Taylor says. "The audience gets to choose the winner."

The crowd in the auditorium begins to get restless. Some people are shouting "Maria," and others are shouting "Tonya." The audience appears to be getting heated. Miss Taylor and the faculty are struggling to keep order. Just as it appears things are going to get out of hand, music starts coming from the piano.

They look up and see Swish is playing the piano. Then he begins to sing. He's singing "What the World Needs Now." "What the World Needs Now Is Love" Swish is singing the lyrics to the song and playing the music and the song on the piano. Everybody starts to watch him.

Then Swish turns towards the audience and says, "Come on everybody sing." Everybody begins singing the song. "Come on one more time," Swish says. "Wave your hands everybody." The whole audience is singing the song now and waving their hands. Then the song ends. Swish gets up off the piano stool. He goes to the center of the stage and takes a bow then goes to sit down.

The crowd gives him a rousing applause and standing ovation. As things quiet down Maria and Tonya walk to the microphone. Maria addresses the audience. "We," Maria says, "Tonya and I agree." Maria looks at Tonya. Tonya nods her head. "We think that Swish should win the competition." First the audience gets quiet. Then Freeze gets up and starts yelling, "Swish!" "Swish!" "Swish!" One by one the entire audience starts yelling "Swish!" "Swish!" "Swish!" This takes place for about five minutes.

Then Miss Taylor goes to the microphone. The auditorium gets quiet. "The people have spoken." Miss Taylor says. "The winner of the 1996 senior talent show is Mr. Benjamin Swisher." The audience breaks out in applause and cheers. Swish gets congratulated as he walks on the stage. People pat him on the head as he goes to accept his award. Now Swish is on stage standing next to Miss Taylor. "Anything you want to say to the audience, Mr. Swisher," Miss Taylor asks him. Swish looks around the room, then he says, "Thank you, everybody." "I love you." The audience yells back "We love you too, Swish."

Swish makes his way over to Freeze and JJ sitting in the judge's box. They both look at Swish and give him a hug. Freeze steps back from Swish. "Where did you learn to sing like that," Freeze asks Swish. Before Swish can answer Freeze says, "I know." "Watching TV, right?" Swish just nods his head up and down. Freeze says, "I gotta find out what channels you be watching."

CHAPTER 12

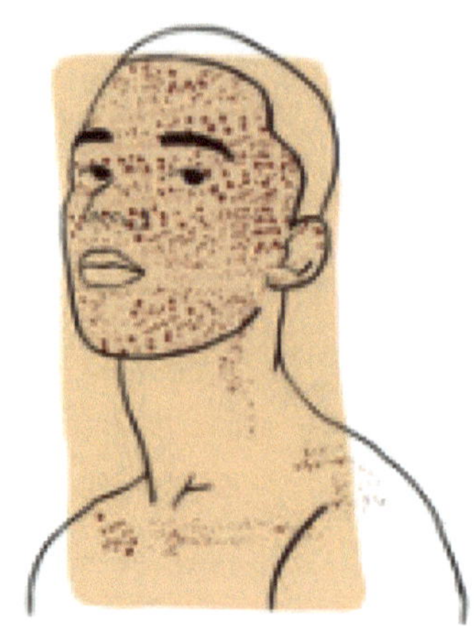

SWISH (BENJI) GETS A DATE FOR THE PROM

Now, it was the last week in May. JJ and Freeze were getting ready for the senior prom. They are both at a tuxedo store shopping for a tuxedo for their senior prom. "Man, these tuxedos are expensive," JJ says. "Yeah, I know." "Especially the blue one I want." Freeze says. "I figured you would wear blue." JJ tells Freeze. As they are looking around Freeze sees Swish sitting in one of the chairs waiting for them.

"Hey, what about Swish?" Freeze says. "What about Swish?" JJ asks. "Well, a tux for him," Freeze says. "He does have two tickets to the prom." Freeze reminds JJ."Yeah." JJ says. "That's true." "But let's face it." JJ says. "Who is going to go to the prom with Swish?" "Just leave that to me." Freeze says. "You really think you can get him a date to the prom?" JJ asks Freeze. "If I can't do it," Freeze says. "My name is, "Attila the Hun." "You know those girls can't resist my irresistible charm." "They will do anything for me." Freeze says. "OK." JJ says. "I'm down wit' it." "Let's go for it."

"First thing first." Freeze says. "Let's get the little man fitted for a tuxedo." "We have to figure out how we're gonna get some money to pay for it." Freeze says. "No, we don't," JJ says. "Oh, you got money to get him a tuxedo?" Freeze asks. "Yeah, I do." JJ answers. "I still got his $1100 from when we won the basketball game in the lower bottoms." JJ says. "You mean you didn't spend that money?" Freeze asks. "No," I didn't spend that money." JJ says. "That's Swish's money." "Would you have spent it?" JJ asks Freeze. Freeze looks at JJ and says, "I take the fifth." JJ stares at Freeze, an evil look. Then Freeze says "Well, I would've thought about it." Now JJ is standing there with his arms crossed and patting his foot. "Ok, ok, I wouldn't have spent it." "Are you satisfied?" He asks JJ. JJ says nothing, he just nods his head. "Man." Freeze says aloud. "Out of all the best friends in the world I could get, I get the son of the Pope."

JJ ignores Freeze comments. "Anyway," JJ says. "Let's get this show on the road. "Right," Freeze says. "Operation Swish in full effect."

The two of them search out a tuxedo for Swish. They have him put on a white one, with a purple sash. "Nice." Freeze says. "You're going to be the life of the party." Freeze says. "Now let's do something about that hair." JJ says. Freeze and JJ go into the store. They find a can of fake hair. "Let's see does this match his color?" They look through the cans of fake hair and find a can of red hair. "Perfect." Freeze says.

They take Swish to get a haircut. Then they take him and buy him some white dress shoes. "Hey man," Freeze says to Swish as he tries on his shoes with his white tuxedo. "You can't be looking more fly than me now." He jokes. "OK, now here's the plan." Freeze says. "I'm gonna find him a date." "You teach him playa etiquette." "Deal." Freeze says. "Deal." JJ says.

The whole week JJ is mentoring Swish on what to say to a young lady while Freeze is trying to get someone to go to the prom with Swish. It's the day before the prom.

"You find someone, Atilla?" JJ asks Freeze. "Nobody," Freeze says. "Not even my mother." "He jokes. "What happened to your irresistible charm?" JJ asks. "Nothing." Freeze says. "I just gotta put it in a little overdrive." Freeze says. "Yeah, I've been asking around to." JJ says. "No luck either." JJ says. "Even offered to pay someone". "Not happening." "I've been rejected in three different languages." JJ says.

Freeze looks over at the basketball court. Kayla Smart is shooting ball. Kayla is the center for the girls' basketball team. She stood 6'2" 180 pounds. She had a tall wiry body. And wore manly clothes. It was hard to tell that she was a female.

Freeze looks at JJ. "Did you ask her?" Freeze asks JJ. "Did I ask who?" JJ inquires. "Her," Freeze says pointing to Kayla. JJ looks over at Kayla. "You talking about her, Kayla?" "King Kong Kayla." "I don't know if you know this or not, but Kayla is not into boys." "She likes girls." JJ says. "I know but we desperate." Freeze says. "Be my guess if you feel bold enough." JJ says ushering Freeze towards Kayla with hand signals.

Freeze walks over to Kayla, who is shooting basketball. "Kayla," Freeze calls her name. Kayla stops dribbling the ball. "What do you want, Freeze?" Kayla answers. "You're pretty good at basketball, huh?" Freeze says. "Get you a squad." Kayla tells Freeze. "Whoa, confident, too." Freeze says. "I love that in a woman," Freeze says. "Me and my girls will beat any team you put on the court." Kayla boasts. JJ whispers in Freeze's ear. "She ain't lying."

"How about one on one." Freeze says. "You don't have nobody male or female at this school that can beat me in basketball." Kayla says. "Not even you." "Because unlike the boys who only won one state championship." Kayla boasts, "The girls have won four state championships." "She right about that." JJ whispers to Freeze.

"I feel ya'." Freeze says. "Tell you what". Freeze says to Kayla. "Seeing that you are physically superior to everybody." "Let's make this a finesse game." "Jump shots only." "My friend here Swish needs a date for the prom." "I hear you were available." "So, here's the deal." Freeze says. "A game of HOP." "You and Swish." "You win, name your price." "We win, you go to the prom as Swish's date."

Kayla looks at Swish and rolls her eyes. "Even if I dated boys." She says, "I damn well sho' wouldn't date no small potatoes like him." "I've had cats bigger than him." Kayla says. "Name yo' price, Kayla?" Freeze says. "Are you scared he's going to beat ya'?" He challenges her. "Tell you what I'll even throw in a fit for you for the prom and I will pay for it," Freeze says. JJ looks at Freeze and says, "We will?" "Yeah," Freeze whispers to JJ. "Remember Swish has money saved up."

"What a better way to spend it on him." Freeze says. JJ says "OK." "Let's go for it."

"Nobody at the school can beat me." Kayla says. "I'm just scared I'm gonna break his little heart." She says as she laughs.

"Name your price." Freeze says. "OK." Kayla says. "If he wins, I will take him to the prom." "What I get if I win?" Kayla says. "You get $500." Freeze says. JJ makes a throat sound and says to Freeze, "Um, um." Then he tugs Freeze's shirt and says, "That's a bit much, isn't it?" JJ whispers to Freeze. "Come on now, JJ." Freeze says. "Have some balls." Freeze tells JJ. "I got this." Freeze assures JJ."Yeah." JJ says. "Last time you told me that, we almost all got killed." JJ reminds Freeze. Freeze says. "I got this," again to JJ. "It's a deal," Kayla says. "OK," Freeze says. "A game of HOP." "Jump shots only." "If Swish wins you take him to the ball." "If you win, we give you $500."

Swish and Kayla meet on the court. A crowd gathers around as Kayla and Swish square off playing a game of HOP. Freeze is holding the ball. He hands the ball to Kayla. "Ladies first." Freeze tells her. Kayla grabs Freeze by the collar. "Don't be playing with me, Freeze." She says, "If I win, I want my $500." Kayla says. "OK, OK, relax queen Zilla." Freeze says. "You're going to get your money if you win." Freeze says standing there with his hands up. Kayla slowly releases his collar.

Kayla takes the first shot. Kayla shoots from the free-throw line. She makes it. The crowd cheers. Swish shoots from the free-throw. He makes it also. The crowd cheers. Kayla shoots from the right corner. She makes it. The crowd cheers. Swish shoots from the right corner. He makes it also. The crowd cheers. Kayla shoots from the left corner. She makes it. The crowd cheers. Swish shoots from the left corner. He makes it also. The crowd cheers. Kayla shoots from the top of the key. She makes it. The crowd cheers. Swish shoots from the top of the key. He makes it also. The crowd cheers. The two of them go back and forth. Each of them making it.

Finally, Kayla goes to the far-right corner. She takes a shot. The ball hits the front of the rim and falls to the court. A groan comes from the crowd. Now for the first time Swish is in control of where the ball is shot from. "Now it is Swish's turn." Freeze says.

Freeze tells Swish, "Go to the top of the key." Swish goes to the top of the key. Swish shoots the ball. It goes straight in. The crowd cheers. Kayla shoots from the top of the key. The ball goes in and the crowd cheers. For another 15 minutes the two exchange shots and both of them make the shot.

"Swish," Freeze calls him over. "This girl is good." He tells Swish. "You gonna have to get creative my friend." "Ok Swish," Freeze says. This time Swish goes to the top of the free-throw line of the other court. "Ooh", the crowd says. "Wait a minute." Kayla says. "Nobody in basketball shoots from there." Kayla complains. "This is not a basketball game Kayla." Freeze says. "This is HOP," he informs her. "Whatever." Kayla says. "I doubt if funny man can make it from there anyway," Kayla says.

Swish goes and steps on the free throw line of the other court. He squares up. Then he heaves the ball. Everyone's eyes follow the trajectory of the arc of the ball. "Swish," is the sound the ball makes as it goes through the net. The crowd erupts in cheers. Now it is Kayla's turn to shoot. She takes the ball to the free throw line of the opposite court. She squares to shoot. The ball is in the air. "Bong," is the sound it makes as it hits the front rim. A groan goes through the crowd. "I believe that's "H"." Freeze says to Kayla.

Swish goes and steps on the top of the key of the other court. He squares up. Then he heaves the ball. Everyone's eyes follow the trajectory of the arc of the ball. "Swish", is the sound of the ball as it goes through the net. The crowd erupts in cheers. Now it is Kayla's turn to shoot. She takes the ball to the top of the key line of the opposite court. She squares up to shoot. The ball is in the air. "Bong" is the sound it makes as it hits the front rim. A groan goes through the crowd. "I believe that's HO." Freeze says to Kayla. "Whatever," Kayla says to Freeze.

Next Swish goes to the out of bounds line of the opposite court. The full length of the court. "Ooh," the crowd says. Swish squares up. And he shoots the ball. The crowd is quiet as they watch the ball go straight into the hoop. Everyone begins cheering. Now, it is Kayla's turn to shoot. She squares up at the line the full distance of the court. She shoots the ball. "Whoosh," is the sound as she airballs. "That's HOP." Freeze says to Kayla as he is taunting her putting his hand in her face hopping around her. Kayla looks frustrated. She swipes at Freeze's hand, but he is too quick and each time she misses. "Well, well." JJ says. Cinderfella is going to the ball." Freeze adds, With the bride of Frankenstein." Freeze and JJ give each other a high five.

Swish walks up to Kayla and gets down on one knee and asks, "Would you go to the prom with me," he says as his hand reaches out to her. The crowd goes "a-a-w." She knocks his hand away and just leaves the court.

Freeze goes to stand by Swish. "That's OK Swish, baby boy." "You got a date for tomorrow night." Freeze assures him. "Be ready at five Kayla." Freeze reminds her. Kayla throws her hands up and keeps walking. She gives Freeze the middle finger. "Aw baby," Freeze says. "Let's not get personal now." Freeze tells her. "Come on Swish." JJ says. "We got to get you ready for the prom tomorrow." JJ and Freeze escort Swish out of the gym.

CHAPTER 13

THE PROM

The last day of May had arrived. May 31. And today was the day of the senior prom. Some ritzy hotel downtown. Most seniors didn't go to school that day. They were preparing for that night. Next to graduation the senior prom is the biggest day of their life so far. Freeze and Swish spent the day at JJ's house. The early part of the day they went out and played basketball. At about noon they went to the burger shop. Freeze and JJ spend some time going over with Swish on how to treat a lady. "Hey it's 1 o'clock." JJ says. "We need to get to the house." "OK", Freeze says "Give me a couple of minutes to finish my shake and I'll be ready." The guys finish up at the burger shop, then head to the bus stop. On the way to JJ's house, they stopped downtown to pick up their tuxedos. They ride the bus downtown to Smith's to get the tuxedos. The boys pick up their tuxedos and head back home.

The time is 3 o'clock when they get back to JJ's home. Freeze decides to take a nap on the couch while JJ goes over some etiquette lessons with Swish. JJ is so entrenched in his lessons with Swish he doesn't keep track of time. Fortunately, he set the alarm clock. The alarm clock goes off at 5:00.

JJ runs to the couch and wakes up Freeze. "Get up," Freeze JJ says. "Time to get dressed." Freeze gets up and goes to take a shower. JJ helps Swish get dressed. Swish undresses down to his underwear. JJ helps him first put on his pants. Then he helps him put on his shirt. JJ goes to make sure that Freeze is up. He comes back down to see about Swish. He looks at Swish standing there. Swish has a black spot on his white pants in the little time he left him alone. "Aw man", JJ yells out. "Swish what did you do to your pants?" "I don't know." Swish says in his childlike voice.

Freeze comes out the bathroom draped in a towel. "OK, what did Swish do?" Freeze inquires. "I heard you all the way upstairs." "He got a dark spot on his pants." JJ complains. "Oh, is that all", Freeze says. "I thought he set the house on fire or something," Freeze says laughing. "Let me get dressed and I can handle that." Freeze assures JJ. "OK," but hurry up," JJ tells Freeze. "The limo will be here any minute."

Freeze gets dressed. Then he looks at the small dark spot on Swish's left pant leg. Freeze says, "Never fear." "Freeze is here." "OK, iceman." JJ says. "What we gonna do about this situation?" Freeze takes a look at the pants. Then he says, "Do you know for a young man," "You sure fret a lot." "Now watch this." Freeze says. "Presto." Freeze pulls a small bottle out of his pocket.

"And what, pray tell, might I ask is that ?" JJ inquires. "This my homie," Freeze says, "Is white out." "Never leave home without it." Freeze informs JJ. Freeze opens the white out and starts applying it to the black dot on Swishes pants until the dark spot can't be seen. "There." Freeze says. "Good as new." He tells JJ.

"And you just happen to have a bottle of white out in your pocket?" JJ asks Freeze. "Sure," Freeze responds. "Never know when it's needed." "Comes in handy." "You might make a mistake on paper." "You might need to change something that you wrote down." JJ interrupts. "You might need to cheat on a test or do graffiti in the school bathrooms." JJ adds. "C'mon now bruh," Freeze says. "That's confidential."

The three young men finish getting dressed. Freeze stands Swish up in front of the mirror. "Look at you, smooth." He tells Swish. "All dressed up." "You clean as a cool summer breeze, boy." Freeze tells him. Swish stands there in the mirror smiling. "Don't worry about who's gonna be King of the prom." "You know that's gonna be me." Freeze says sporting his blue tuxedo with his blue cool daddy hat on. "You do understand that I am going to be king of the ball," he tells Swish. Swish says, "Uh huh." As he nods his head.

"See my man." Freeze says to Swish. "With answers like that you're gonna be my friend for a long time." Freeze says. A big grin comes on Swish's face. "Hey, JJ." Freeze says, as he gets JJ's attention. "Look at my man here, Swish." "Ain't he the coolest cat you ever seen?" JJ is in another mirror fixing his tie. He glances over quickly at Swish and Freeze.

"Yeah, Freeze," JJ answers. "He is sharp as a tack." JJ says. Then he goes back to fixing his tie. Just then they hear a horn blow. "Limo's here," Freeze says to JJ. The three young men gather their things and head out to the limousine. They are going to meet their dates at Freeze's girlfriend's house, Rebecca Charles. JJ's date is Joyce Powell. And of course, Kayla is Swish's date.

They arrive at Rebecca's house at about 5:30. JJ and Freeze run up the stairs and ring the doorbell. Rebecca's mother opens the door and greets them. "You young men have a seat right here on the couch and the girls will be down shortly," she says. When she walked away, Freeze tells JJ, "I told you they wouldn't be on time." "Yeah," JJ says, "It's like an unwritten rule for women, huh." JJ tells Freeze. "More like it's in their DNA," Freeze says. Freeze gives a high five to JJ."

The first one down the steps is Joyce. As she sauntered down the steps the young men can't take their eyes off her. How stunningly beautiful she is in her lavender dress. "Hello gentlemen." She says politely. The young men stand there and admire her beauty.

Next down the stairs is Rebecca. She floats down the stairs in her pink dress. Once again, the boys gawk at her beauty. "Welcome to my home." She tells them. "Kayla will be down shortly," she informs them. Five minutes go by. Still the boys haven't said a word. Just sitting there with their eyes wide open.

Next Kayla comes down the stairs. Kayla is wearing a white chiffon dress. She is a little unsteady on her feet in that she is not used to wearing high heels. The boys are really stunned at her beauty. Until this time they considered Kayla was one of the boys. Tall and slender and very attractive. "Never thought Kayla would look so good." Freeze thought in his mind.

As soon as he saw Kayla, Swish jumped up and met her at the bottom of the steps. "It is my pleasure, sweet princess to be taking you to the prom," Swish tells her. He gets down on one knee and asks her, "Would you allow me to put this corsage around your ankle," Swish asks Kayla. "Whatever." Kayla says.

Swish puts the corsage around Kayla's right ankle. Rebecca and Joyce look at JJ and Freeze expectantly. "Well,"Rebecca says to Freeze. "Well, what?" Freeze answers. Rebecca crosses her arms and says, "Do I get a corsage?" "Oh yeah," Freeze says. He pulls his corsage out of his bag and hands it to her. She takes a deep breath and looks down at her ankle. "Oh yeah." Freeze says. He gets down on one knee and puts the corsage on Rebecca's right ankle.

Now it's Joyce's turn. She looks at JJ. JJ looks puzzled. Then Joyce looks down at her ankle. "Oh yeah." JJ says. He pulls out his corsage and puts it on Joyce's ankle. "Girl." Rebecca tells Joyce. "Who would have thought that the slow guy was gonna be the most romantic one tonight." "I'm telling you girl," Rebecca says to Joyce as they high-fived each other.

"OK ladies." Freeze says. "Our chariot is waiting." The limousine is a stretch white vehicle. Freeze and JJ run out to the limousine leaving everyone else behind. "May I escort you my princess to the limousine?" Swish asks Kayla. "Oh, Negro please." Kayla tells Swish. "I can walk by myself." "Thank you anyway." She says with an attitude.

The four of them who have been left behind make it to the limousine. JJ and Freeze are already inside when they get to it. Swish walks ahead of the group of ladies. He opens the limo door for Kayla. Kayla just nods her head to him and gets in. Rebecca and Joyce stand outside the limousine. Rebecca makes a throat clearing sound as if to give the guys a hint. Then JJ finally gets the hint. He jumps out the car and opens the door for Joyce. He is followed by Freeze who gets out of the car and opens the door for Rebecca.

"Are you sure that you guys taught Swish the ropes, or did Swish teach you guys the ropes?" Rebecca says. "Come on Rebecca, baby." Freeze says. "I'm just excited to see you." Freeze tells her. "I just slipped up a little bit." Freeze says.

JJ also chimes in. "Yeah Joyce, you girls are stunningly beautiful today." "We have never seen you girls dressed up like this." JJ says "OK." Rebecca says. "But I hope the rest of the night goes better than this." "Relax." Freeze says, "Drinks are on me." "Look here you got Dr. Pepper, Pepsi,7-Up and Coke." He says opening up the cold box in the limo. Freeze pops open a soda and starts drinking it and the limo pulls off on the way to their destinations.

The limousine pulls up to the hotel. Once again Swish gets out and opens the door for Kayla. Freeze and JJ follow suit. They get out and open the door for the ladies they are escorting. "Swish puts his hand out to help Kayla out the car. Kayla pushes his hand out the way. Rebecca and Joyce are being assisted out of the car by Freeze and JJ. Rebecca tells Kayla,"Girl you better recognize a good thing when you see it." Kayla says, "If you think he's so good you take him." " Naw girl." Rebecca says. "Unfortunately, I made a commitment to Bozo here."

The six of them enter the Plaza. The music is already blasting. They present their tickets to the maître d'. He leads them to their table which is close to the door. When they get to the table Swish pulls a chair out from under the table for Kayla to sit in. She reluctantly takes a seat. He begins to take a seat next to her. "Please." Kayla says. "Please don't sit next to me." Kayla tells Swish "Yes, my princess." Swish says. Swish goes and stands up next to the dance floor. He stands next to some support beams and leans on them.

"Man, Kayla." Freeze says. "You kinda of being harsh on my man." Kayla says, "I agreed to come to the prom with him." "That's it." She says in a defiant voice. "Lighten up Kayla." JJ says. "Come on the little guy is sensitive." "You might hurt his feelings." JJ reminds her. Kayla with her arms folded just sits in a chair. "Whatever," Kayla says.

Meanwhile there seems to be some excitement over on the dance floor. "Let's go check it out." Freeze says. "Come on Kayla let's go check it out." Rebecca encourages her. Kayla just throws her right hand up rejecting them.

They (JJ, Freeze, Rebecca, and Joyce) go check out the dance floor. They have to wade through a crowd to make it to the dance floor. When they get to the dance floor they are in shock. Swish is on the dance floor doing every dance from the "Chubby Checker, Twist" to the "Michael Jackson, "Moonwalk." Everybody is yelling, "Go Swish!" "Go Swish!" "Go Swish!" "Go Swish!"

Somebody yells, "Electric slide, electric slide!"

Swish leads the whole group in the electric slide. "Are you seeing this?" Freeze asks JJ. JJ says. "Pinch me." "I gotta be dreaming." After they were done doing the electric slide all the girls wanted to dance with Swish. After four hours on the dance floor the band took a break. Everyone went to take a seat at their tables.

"Where is Swish?" Rebecca asks. "I don't know?" Freeze says. "Maybe he went to the bathroom." JJ says. "I'll go check." Just when JJ starts to get up a voice comes from the stage. It's Swish. JJ sits down after he hears Swish's voice on the microphone.

"This is for the young lady that I was so graced to come to the prom with." Swish says. "I am not even worthy to drink out of her slipper." Swish says. "Kayla my princess." Swish says. "This is for you."

Then he walks off stage playing a guitar and goes into a rendition of the Righteous Brothers "Unchained Melody." And he begins to sing in a sensuous smooth voice. "Oh my love, my darling." All the girls begin to scream and run toward the stage. Some of them throw their corsages at him. Kayla is just looking starry eyed as Swish is singing to her. Swish slowly descends from the stage playing the guitar, serenading Kayla as he is walking from the stage towards her. He walks towards Kayla who is sitting down mesmerized. The crowd departs like Moses departing the Red Sea to make a path to let Swish through. On his way to Kayla Swish pulls one of the roses from one of the flower displays in the room. He slowly walks towards Kayla. All eyes are on Swish and Kayla. As Swish makes it to Kayla he goes down on one knee. And he hands her the rose he has picked. By now tears are coming out of Kayla's eyes. She pulls him up to his feet and lets him sit next to her. Swish holds her hand. Kayla just sits there looking at Swish starry eyed.

The band returns to the dance floor. "OK ladies and gentlemen." "Time for the last song." "If you got to get on the dance floor now is the time." The bandleader says.

Fifteen to twenty girls line up at Swish's table hoping that he was going to do the last dance with them. To their demise Kayla stands up and says, "Excuse me, ladies." "This is my date." All the young ladies quickly back away from the table. No one wants any parts of King Kong Kayla.

Kayla gets up to walk, but she stumbles a bit since she is not used to high heels. Swish gently helps her sit down and they take her shoes off.

Then Swish escorts Kayla to the dance floor.

When they get to the dance floor couples are dancing on the dance floor to "Ribbon in the Sky" by "Stevie Wonder." You couldn't help but notice the short Swish dancing with a tall Kayla. But they were so smooth together. So, everyone on the dance floor ceded to this couple on the dance floor dancing to "Ribbon in the Sky" by "Stevie Wonder." The music ended with Swish swinging Kayla around and catching her in his arms.

The students cheered as the music ended. Everyone goes to have a seat at their tables as cake and punch are served. Kayla was sitting next to Swish now. She couldn't take her eyes off of him. Someone walks up on stage. It was Jason Torres, school student body president.

"Okay ladies and gentlemen," he says. "Before we leave." "Here are the results of the king and queen of the prom." "The most exciting couple of the 1996 Amanda Ellen Thompkins High School prom of 1996 is," there's a drumroll,then Jason Torres announces the two names. "Kayla Smart, and Benjamin Swisher."

First everyone is quiet. Then Freeze jumps up on his feet and starts yelling, "Swish!" "Swish!" "Swish!" Then everyone starts yelling "Swish!" "Swish!" "Swish!" as Swish and Kayla make it up to the podium. They are crowned king and queen of the prom. "Come on say a few words," Jason Torres tells the two of them.

First Kayla gets up there. Kayla thanks the crowd for the honor. She tells them how she had never intended to come to the senior prom and how she had had the best time of her life.

Then they hand the microphone to Swish. Everyone gets quiet. Swish looks around at the crowd. Then Swish says in his timid voice, "I love everybody, and I just want everybody to be my friend." The crowd is silent.

Then, Freeze says, "We love you too, Swish!" Then everybody starts saying, "We love you too Swish!" Then they carry Swish off the stage back to his seat. The crowd starts again "Swish! "Swish!" Swish!"

The festivities wrap-up and the young people start back to the parking lot back to their limos. The six of them get into the white limo that is waiting for them. This time JJ and Freeze quickly open the door for their dates. Swish has already opened the door for Kayla, and they are sitting in the back of the limo. JJ and Joyce are sitting in the center and Freeze and Rebecca are sitting up front. They first get to Kayla's house. They drop Kayla off.

"Goodbye Swish," Kayla says, giving him a kiss on the cheek. "Goodbye my princess." Swish says jumping out of the limo opening the door for her. "Goodbye Kayla." They all say. Kayla takes a couple steps then she turns back to the limo.

"Oh," Kayla says, opening the back of the limousine. "I forgot something." "What did you forget, Kayla?" Rebecca asks. "I forgot this." She says as she grabs Swish by the arm and pulls him out of the car.

Then she slams the car door. "Don't wait up for him." Kayla tells them as she literally drags Swish to her house.

"Bye, Swish." The two girls say in unison. Swish waves goodbye as he is being pulled by Kayla to her house. "Bye, Swish," The girls say again in unison. "Oh boy." Freeze says. "What he got that I don't have?" JJ says. "I don't know." Rebecca says, "But I wish I could find out." "Yeah girl," Joyce says, "Kayla is lucky tonight." Rebecca and Joyce say giving each other a high five. "I'm telling you women." JJ says shaking his head.

The next house they get to is Rebecca's house. Rebecca and Joyce both get out. Joyce is spending the night with Rebecca. "Good night ladies." JJ and Freeze say. Now Freeze and JJ are alone with the driver in the limousine.

"Man that was some crazy ass night." Freeze says to JJ. JJ is quiet at first. Then JJ speaks his mind. "Tell me the truth now, Freeze," JJ says. "Tell you the truth about what?" Freeze asks JJ. "The truth about how you feel about Swish." "You are a little jealous of him, aren't you?" "I mean he stole your thunder." JJ says. Freeze stops and thinks. Then he says, "Why would I be jealous of Swish?" JJ says, "C'mon, Freeze." "All this year you've been talking about being the prom king." "And you know you are always the life of every party." "Swish took that away from you tonight." JJ says. Freeze looks at JJ and says, "You know normally you would be right." "But actually, I'm cool wit' it." "Not being prom king was worth seeing Swish being happy." Freeze says.

"Are you fo' real?" JJ says. "Yeah, I'm fo' real." Freeze says. "Wow," JJ says. "You have changed." JJ says. "That's a good thing, right?" Freeze asks JJ. JJ nods his head. The limousine drives up to JJ's house and JJ and Freeze get out and go into the house.

The next morning it was about 12 noon when JJ got up. He went downstairs and Freeze was still sleeping on the couch. JJ shook Freeze but he was unable to arouse him. JJ went to look in the cupboard for some cereal. He hears a car horn blow. JJ went to the door still dressed in his boxer shorts and T-shirt. He opens the door and there is Swish getting out of the car with Kayla. "Bye, Swish." Kayla says to Swish as she blows him a kiss goodbye. Swish turns around and blows her a kiss back. Swish walks up to the house. He has a big grin on his face.

"Well, Swish", JJ says when Swish approaches him on the porch. "How was your night?" JJ asks Swish. Swish doesn't say anything. He just walks by JJ with a big grin on his face. He walks in and just has a seat on the love seat across from Freeze who is still sleeping. "Well Swish, what you do last night?" Swish just sits there smiling. "You went over Kayla's?" Swish just nods his head. "You get in bed with her?" JJ asks Swish. Swish doesn't say a word he just nods his head smiling. "You went to sleep with her?" JJ asks. Swish just nods his head still smiling. JJ stops and thinks. Then he says, "Ooh Swish, you mean you...," before he could get it out Swish starts nodding his head vigorously with a big grin on his face.

JJ says. "Swish, you are a naughty boy." Swish nods his head even more vigorously. "Wait till I tell Freeze." Freeze wakes up yawning at the sound of his name. "Wait till you tell Freeze what?" Freeze asks between yawns. "Wait till I tell you who's not a virgin anymore before we are." JJ says. "Who my boy Swish?" Freeze says. "I know that Swish got down with Kayla." Freeze says. "How do you know? JJ says."

"C'mon now, JJ you're not that naïve, are you? The girl came and practically drug him out the car like a caveman drags his woman." "What else you think she was coming back to get him for?" "To serve him milk and cookies?" "Look at you Baby Boi!" Freeze says. "Come on over here my man and give yo potna some dap." Swish walks over and gives Freeze a fist pound.

Then Freeze looks at JJ and says, "And speak for yourself homeboy." Freeze says. "My flytrap been sprung a long time ago." JJ looks over at Freeze and says, "Really." "I guess I'm the only gumby around here then."

Freeze puts his arm around Swish. "Welcome to manhood, Mr. Swisher." Freeze tells Swish. "We gonna have to get our friend over there laid so he won't be so uptight." Freeze tells Swish. "Okay." "Okay" Swish says. "Now that you are a man like me," Freeze says looking at JJ. "What can I get you?" Freeze asks Swish. "Some ice cream." Swish says. "You are the man." Freeze tells Swish. "Ice cream it is, on me." "Come on, Mr. Swisher." Freeze puts his arm around Swish.

"You don't mind if this child comes along with us?" Freeze says pointing to JJ. "Whatever." JJ says as they leave out the door. On the way to get ice cream, Freeze asks Swish, "Where you learn to get down with a woman?" "Don't tell me TV?" Freeze asks Swish. Swish shakes his head, "No". "Oh, I was gonna say." Freeze says. "Oh,I was getting ready to say, I, I'm gonna start spending more time at your house watching TV with you."

Freeze puts his arm around Swish's shoulder and JJ puts his arm around his other shoulder as they walk him (to) the ice cream shop.

After they leave the ice cream shop the two walk Swish home. On their way back JJ says, "Can you believe that Swish got down with Kayla." Freeze says, "Yeah that is an unbelievable thought that Kayla got down with any boy, yet alone Swish." A few minutes go by then JJ says, "Do you think you could get down with a girl who likes girls?" He asks Freeze. Freeze answers, "Her sister and her partner all at the same time." Freeze says laughing. "I should've known better than to ask you this question." "You are a pervert." JJ Tells Freeze. "Yeah," Freeze says. "I'm gonna to be a pervert till I'm a deadvert." Freeze says laughing.

Then Freeze looks at JJ and says, "Race you to your place." "Alright." JJ says. They get into a starting position. Freeze begins to count. "Ready on three," Freeze says. "One, three," Freeze says as he takes off running. JJ just stands there shaking his head. Then he runs off after him.

CHAPTER 14

SOMETHING IS WRONG

It is now a week after the prom, six days to go till graduation. JJ is outside watering the lawn. "Hey stranger." Freeze says as he walks up to JJ. "Haven't seen you since two hours ago in class." Freeze jokes. "What's up my homie," JJ says. The two give each other a fist pound and a manly hug. "Hey, you wanna go and play some video games?" JJ asks Freeze. "Sure, why not." Freeze says. "I don't have nothing but time to kill." "C'mon in here so I can school you young fella," JJ says. "Not in this lifetime," Freeze says.

The two get the video games out. They set it up and begin playing. As they are playing Freeze asks, "How is our little playboy doing?" "I miss the little fella." Freeze says. JJ responds. "Who, Swish?" "I don't know." "I miss him, too." "I haven't seen him in two or three days." Last time I spoke to his mother she said he needed to get some rest and she was going to keep him in a few days.

They continue to play their video games. They have been playing video games about an hour when the phone rings. JJ stops the game. "What are you stopping the game for? "I was winning." Freeze says. "Phone ringing," JJ says. "It might be Moms." JJ runs to get the phone. "Okay," Freeze says. "Don't let that be the reason you lose." Freeze tells JJ.

JJ hangs up the phone with a puzzled look on his face. "Who dat' was?" Freeze asks. "That was Swish's Mama." JJ answers. "What's up with Swish?" "He Okay?" Freeze asks. "Don't know," JJ answers. "His mama says he is in the hospital." "She says he has relapsed." JJ informs Freeze.

"What does that mean?" JJ asks. "I don't know?" Freeze says. "What hospital is he at?" Freeze asks. "County General," JJ answers. "Let's go see about my little homie." Freeze says.

The two catch the bus to the east side of town. Both sat joking around trying not to show how worried they were. "County General." The driver yells out. "Here's our stop." JJ says nudging Freeze who is almost gone to sleep. They both exit the bus. "Man, what could be wrong with my little sidekick?" JJ says. "Don't fret." Freeze says. "He's a trooper." "He's gonna be alright." "That's a strong little dude." Freeze assures JJ. They reach the front of the hospital entrance and approach the front desk. A hefty Black lady dressed in all white with a nurse's cap sat at the front desk.

Freeze approaches her and says, "I come to see Swish—." He catches himself, "I mean Benjamin Swisher." Freeze tells the lady. She looks up the name on her clipboard. Then looks over her black brim glasses and eyes the two of them. "And who, might you be?" She asks them. "We are friends of his." JJ says. The lady looks down on her board and looks back up. "Sorry," she says. "Family only.

"But ma'am," JJ says. "You don't understand his mother——"Family only," she says cutting him off. "Lady don't you have no heart." Freeze says. "Young man don't you have any ears?" "Family only." The lady repeats herself while pointing her fat stubby finger towards the exit. Both turn and exit the hospital.

JJ begins to descend the stairs. Freeze grabs his left shoulder and stops him. "She can't do that." Freeze says. "Looks like she can to me." JJ responds. "Come on now I know you not going out like that?" Freeze says to JJ. "Yeah, what do you suggest?" Freeze whispers into JJ's ear.

Both of them enter back into the hospital. Freeze nudges JJ then walks up to the desk. The lady looks up from the magazine she is reading. "Oh, you again." "Family only, I said." The lady says. "I know ma'am," Freeze replies. "But I gots to pee," he says, jumping around like he had ants in his pants. "Well, I suggest you go home young man." The lady says. "C'mon lady", Freeze begs. "Home is a 30-minute bus ride away." "Too bad," she says. "Now outta here." She commands them. "Okay." Freeze answers. "Guess I am gonna have to take a whiz right here," he insists. He unzips his pants. "Young man." The woman gasps holding her bosom. "Okay lady what is it." The bathroom or a new floor job?" Freeze says. "Okay," she says as she cedes. "The bathroom then off be with you." She tells Freeze as she buzzes the door and the two begin to enter.

"Uh-uh." "You, only." She motions for Freeze. JJ looks at Freeze. He just shakes his head. "Plan B." Freeze whispers to JJ. Freeze enters and starts down the hallway towards the bathroom. The lady watches Freeze as he enters the bathroom then turns her attention on JJ who is standing by the door. The lady keeps a suspicious watch on JJ. "I got my eye on the two of you," she says. "Y'all up to no good." The two stand there for about three minutes watching each other. "One thing for sure, lady." JJ says. She looks at him with an attitude. "You can't watch the both of us at the same time." JJ says. Just as he says it Freeze reaches over and presses the door release. A loud buzzer sounds and JJ darts through the door.

"Security, security," the lady yells as she hits them with all types of thrown objects. "Relax, lady." Freeze says as he dodges everything from books, to papers, to pens and pencils. As JJ comes through the door both run down the hallway to the elevator. They wait on what seemed hours for the elevator as the lady at the front desk calls for security. "Ding," the elevator came just as security got to the front desk. The boys saw the lady pointing in their direction. Security hurriedly came towards them. "Hurry in the elevator." Freeze tells JJ shoving him in the elevator. He quickly closes the door and pushes a floor just as a security person reaches the elevator.

The elevator ascends. "Now what?" JJ asks Freeze. "Relax, buddy." "Don't you have confidence in me?" Freeze asks JJ. "Okay, what's the plan?" JJ asks. "We need to find out what room Swish is in." Freeze says. "Really, now that's a novel thought." "You think of that all by yourself," JJ says sarcastically.

The elevator door opens. "Come on." Freeze whispers as he pulls JJ out of the elevator. The two are looking in the doors down the hall each way. A noise comes from the end of the hallway. It is security looking for them. Freeze grabs JJ by the arm and pulls him into a janitor's closet. Security passes them up. "Why is it every time I'm with you it seems I'm running for my life," JJ asks Freeze.

"That's because you have a boring life." Freeze says. "And I put some spice into it." "Yeah," JJ says, "Well put a little more sugar and a little less pepper, please." JJ requests. "Okay." Freeze says as he peeps out the closet. "Coast is clear, JJ." "Let's make our move." Freeze says. The two ease out the closet. Just as they felt they had gotten away, a towering, tall security man showed up. They turn to run the other way only to run into another security guard. "Yeah, you two troublemakers." The other guy says. "All right come on with us." The guy says.

"You don't understand." JJ says. "Our friend is here; he is very sick." "We just want to see him." JJ explains. "Yeah, yeah sure," the security guard says. "Don't bother to try to reason with these marks." Freeze says. "They were born with no hearts." Just at that time someone calls their names.

"Foster, Jenkins," a lady's voice is heard. The two young men look up to see Swish's mother standing in the doorway of one of the rooms. "Is there a problem Officer?" Miss Swisher asks the security guard. "You know these two?" The security guard asks Miss Swisher. "Yes, I know these two," Miss Swisher says. "They are good friends with my son." "I have my son's doctor's permission to let them come see him." She tells the officers.

The tall security guard looks at the other guard. He nods his head. "Yes, ma'am if you can vouch for them." The officer says handing the two boys over to her. "Thank you, sir." Miss Swisher tells the security officer.

The security officers are now leaving. Freeze jumps at the officers like he's going to do something physical. "Would you stop," JJ says. "Don't mess it up." JJ tells Freeze. "We in." "Yeah," Freeze says. "He didn't know who he is messing wit'." Freeze says as he looks at JJ and takes his thumb across his nose. JJ says, "You know I'm gonna get you some professional help when we get out of here." "Oh, an NFL contract." Freeze says. He looks at JJ and JJ shakes his head. "Well, you said professional help." "How much more professional than the NFL can you get?" Freeze says.

"Come this way young men." Miss Swisher says to them. The young men walk into a room. Lying in the bed is Swish. He has all types of tubes and gadgets making beeping noises coming out of him and hooked up to him. "Is he okay?" Freeze asks Miss Swisher. Miss Swisher says, "I'm afraid not, Mr. Foster,". "You see, Benji has leukemia." "He's been dealing with it for five years now." "I don't want to lie to you boys." "He is not gonna be with us long." She tells them.

Both JJ and Freeze look at each other in shock. Freeze then grabs Miss Swisher's hand and just holds it. "Can he say anything?" JJ asks. "You can try." Miss Swisher says. "He has been in and out of it."

JJ walks to the bed next to Swish. "Hey buddy." "Can you hear me." JJ says as he keeps trying to arouse Swish. After five minutes Swish slowly opens his eyes. "A big grin comes on his face when he sees JJ. "Hi." Swish says." Swish asks, "Are you my friend?" JJ grabs Swish's hand and says, "Yes, Swish, I am your friend." "And Freeze is here." "He's your friend too."

Freeze comes over and grabs Swish's other hand. A big grin comes on Swish's face. " Are you my friend?" Swish asks Freeze. Freeze says, "Yes, Swish."

"I am your friend, too." Freeze says. "Friends for life," JJ says. JJ put his hand out to give Swish a fist pound. A feeble Swish puts his hand out to fist pound JJ's hand. Freeze puts his hand out to get a fist pound and Swish gives him a fist pound.

"I'm here for you buddy." Freeze says. A big grin comes on Swish's face. Then he goes back to sleep. "Okay, boys." Miss Swisher says. "Let my boy get some rest." The two boys turn around and give Miss Swisher an embrace. "I want to tell you young men," she tells JJ and Freeze. "I appreciate what you have done for my boy." She says, "You made these the happiest days of his life."

"No, Miss Swisher." Freeze says. "However, much we did for your boy; It will never match what he did for us." "He made these the happiest days of our lives." Freeze says. JJ nods to her.

The two of them head off downstairs and they run into the lady at the front desk. "Next time," she says in a sharp stinging voice. They look up at her with their sad faces. She stops saying what she was getting ready to say sensing their sadness. "God bless you two," she says instead. They just walk by her without saying a word.

As they leave out the exit Freeze looks at JJ. "Hey, JJ," Freeze says in a low-key voice. "Yeah, Freeze." JJ says in an even sadder voice. "Would you think less of me if I cried right now?" Freeze asks JJ. JJ just shakes his head side to side. "I was about to ask you the same thing." JJ says to Freeze. The two, sit on a bench and they begin to weep. Two days later Swish passed away.

CHAPTER 15

RETURN TO THE LOWER BOTTOMS

The morning after Swish died was Saturday morning. Freeze came over JJs house. JJ was still in the bed. Freeze is trying to get his friend out the bed. "Get up hood rat." Freeze says as he shakes JJ trying to get him up. "Leave me alone." JJ says as he turns over in the bed putting the cover over his head. Freeze snatches the cover off of JJ. "Come on JJ get up." Freeze says. "Man, you are annoying." JJ tells Freeze. "Why don't you just disappear?" JJ tells Freeze. "Nope, you ain't gonna get rid of me that easy." Freeze says. "Come on we got something to do." Freeze says. JJ sits up in the bed rubbing the sleep out of his eyes. "What now?" "And how did you get in the house?" JJ asks. "Oh, moms, was leaving just as I came." "She let me in." Freeze says. "I'm gonna have to have a long talk with moms." JJ says.

"Aw quit, you so crazy." Freeze says. "Come on I got a plan." Freeze says. "Oh, God." JJ says. "Here we go." "Another one of your crazy schemes," JJ says. "What we doing this time, Freeze?" JJ asks. "Get up and get dressed," Freeze says. "And I'll tell you on the way."

JJ gets up and gets dressed. He meets Freeze who is waiting outside with a basketball. They start walking down the street. "Okay, what are we going to do?" JJ asks Freeze. "We are going to the lower bottoms to earn some money." Freeze says. "I'm outta here." JJ says as he turns around and starts back home.

"Come on, JJ." Freeze pleads. JJ is now back pedaling talking to Freeze. JJ says, "Are you serious?" "We just almost got killed down there." "Ain't no money that important." JJ tells Freeze. "I'm not getting the money for me." Freeze says. "I'm getting the money for Miss Swisher." Freeze tells JJ.

JJ stops. "You getting the money for Miss Swisher?" JJ inquires. "Yeah Fam, for Miss Swisher." Freeze repeats himself. "Wow", JJ says. "What a nice thing to do," JJ says as he slowly walks back towards Freeze. JJ has made it back to Freeze. "Okay, two things." "What's the plan and who we gonna have as our third person, JJ asks? "You worry too much." Freeze says. "I got this." Freeze tells JJ. "Yeah, last time you said you got this you really got this." "I ended up running like Jesse Owens in the Olympics and you almost ended up hamburger meat," JJ says. Just then they hear someone calling their names.

They look up and Big Mo, the center from the high school basketball team is coming up the street. "Didn't I tell you I got this?" Freeze tells JJ. The three greet each other with an embrace.

"Hey fellas." Big Mo says." "I'm all in." "Anything for Lil Swish my little potna dude." Big Mo says kissing his index finger and pointing it to the sky. "That was a great little guy." JJ says, I'm in." JJ says. "But this time, I'm not abandoning you." JJ tells Freeze. Freeze says, "We ride together." JJ says, "We die together." All three of them say, "I am my brother's keeper." "I feel ya," Freeze says. The three head off to the lower bottoms.

They go to the basketball courts on the lower bottoms. All eyes are on them. A lot of the guys remember them from the last time they were there. Freeze looks around. He sees two familiar faces. He points them out.

"Those are the two guys who jumped me." Freeze tells them. "So, what we gonna do?" JJ asks. "Well for one we gonna stick together." "And leave the rest to me." Freeze says. "Okay." JJ says. "You remember what happened last time we left the rest to you." "You ended up in the hospital." JJ reminds Freeze. "Relax, JJ." Freeze says. "I got this." JJ looks in the sky as if he were praying then he gives Freeze that okay, I'm depending on you look.

The basketball games begin. Just as before the guy in black collects the money from them. "$200 this time. "The guy says. "The stakes are higher this time." He informs Freeze. Freeze hands the man ten $20 bills.

The games go as last time. JJ and his team have swept through the other teams to the last game. They have already earned $2000. The final pot has $4000 in it. If they win that they will walk away with $6000. Again there's a break in the action.

During the break Freeze huddles up with his team and whispers in their ears. He tells them what they're going to do after the game is over. The final game starts. JJ and his team get off to a slow start. They are trailing 16 to 10, but now Freeze and JJ get hot. Now the score is 20 to 20.

Now that the two guards are hot the other team can no longer double guard Big Mo in the middle as they have been doing. Freeze and JJ feed Big Mo under the basket. Big Mo scores the last four points and JJ and his team have won. They go collect their money.

The guy with the toothpick in his mouth slowly counts out $6000 in 20s. Once he finishes counting the money to them; they go to leave. They turn around to face about eight guys who have surrounded them.

"You punks think you can come over here on our side of town and strip us, you got us twisted." This big guy with a patch over his eye says as he flicks out a knife. Several other of the guys flick out knives, too.

The three guys, Big Mo, JJ, and Freeze stand together in solidarity. "Hey Freeze." A voice comes from afar. In a distance six guys wielding baseball bats are approaching. The guys that have surrounded them turn to see who is coming. It is Slim and Big Baby and four other guys. All of them are wielding baseball bats.

"Hey, Slim." Freeze says. "What brings you to this part of town?" Slim says. "I was trying to get a baseball team together." "There are only six of us." "I need you three." Slim says. They walk through the guys that have JJ and Freeze and Big Mo surrounded. Slim walks up to Freeze and the two embrace.

Slim looks at the guys who are surrounding JJ and Freeze and Big Mo. "Hey ladies." Slim says waving the bat in his hands. "Why don't you get your guys together and play my guys in baseball?" Slim tells them. One by one the group surrounding them starts to walk off.

"What?" Slim says. "Y'all don't like baseball?" "Man, that's un-American." Slim says.

Freeze and Slim look at each other again. They embrace each other. "Man I didn't ever think I would be glad to see yo' ugly face." Freeze says to Slim. "Oh, yeah," Slim says. "Yo' girlfriend likes it." Slim says rubbing his hand across his face. "Well, am I still an asshole?" Slim asks Freeze. Freeze says, "Yeah, you are an asshole." Slim steps back and looks at Freeze with a funny look on his face. "But you're a good asshole." Freeze says. "I will take that." Slim says. "That's progress."

All the young men greet each other. Then Slim says, "Let's get you out of here safely." "We're gonna walk all the way through these parts with you till you get to our side of town." Slim says.

Freeze shows Slim how much money they made. "Okay, we got $6000." "We can share $3000 with you and your guys." "But the other $3000 we got to give to Miss Swisher." Freeze tells Slim.

Slim looks at the money and says, "Normally my commission is 20%." "But this is for lil man." "Me and my boys pass." "Matter fact we gonna add to the pot." Slim says. Each of the guys with Slim gives Freeze $20. JJ and Freeze and Big Mo are escorted by Slim and his crew until they make it back to their hood.

Everybody says their goodbyes and goes their separate ways. JJ and Freeze take the money they have gotten and take it to Miss Swisher. "I don't know how to thank you." Miss Swisher tells them. "This will pay the cost of his funeral." "Now all I have to do is raise money for his plot." She tells them.

"What do you want us to do?" Freeze says. Miss Swisher says, "You two have done enough." "Thank you very much." "I will have to figure this out, myself." Miss Swisher tells the boys. Freeze and JJ leave after they give Miss Swisher an embrace.

On the way walking Freeze mocks Miss Swisher. "You two have done enough." "To hell we have." "We need to get the job done." "Who does she think she is?" Freeze huffs. JJ says, "I believe she is his mother." "The person that gave birth to him." JJ reminds Freeze.

"Doesn't matter." Freeze says. "Once I start a job, I finish it." "She needs our help, and dammit' she's gonna get it whether she wants it or not." Freeze says. JJ says, "Okay, superman." "What do you suggest?" JJ says. "I suggest we take a collection at school." Freeze says. "OK." JJ says. "Let's get started, Monday morning."

It is now Monday morning. JJ and Freeze are asking their classmates to give donations for Swish's services. At about noon Mr. Johnson calls them in the office. The two young men go to Mr. Johnson's office.

"You two young men have a seat." Mr. Johnson says. The two have a seat. Both of them trying to figure out what they have done. Mr. Johnson says, "I hear you two are doing an unauthorized fundraiser activity at the school." JJ looks at Freeze and Freeze looks at JJ. Freeze says, "Mr. Johnson we're just trying to raise money for Swish's funeral." Mr. Johnson looks at Freeze and says, "Well on the record young men, it is my duty to tell you gentlemen that unauthorized fundraising is not allowed on school grounds." "Do you guys understand?" Mr. Johnson informed them.

"Yes sir, Mr. Johnson," they both say in unison. "We will stop." JJ says. Then Mr. Johnson says, "Now that I've done that, off the record you gentleman are doing a fantastic job." "Here's my $20 donation to Swish's fundraiser." "And if anybody asks you, I don't know anything about it." They look at each other with big grins on their faces. "Yes sir, Mr. Johnson" they both say as they leave the office.

By the end of the day the two have raised another $6000 including donations from Swish's teachers. At the end of school day, they take the money to Swish's mother. She was so appreciative of their efforts. She tells them, "Now, boys I only need $3000 of this, you can take the other $3000 back." Freeze looks at Miss Swisher and says, "Look Miss Swisher, in all due respect." "We raised this $6000 for you, and if it's alright with you we gonna leave this extra $3000 with you." "What you do wit it is up to you." Freeze tells her. Freeze looks around the house. "Looks like you need a new couch, or some new drapes." "It's up to you, but the extra $3000 is yours ma'am." Miss Swisher looks at JJ. JJ throws his hands up in the air. "Sorry, ma'am." JJ says. "He's stubborn like that."

Miss Swisher smiles and says, "You boys are saints." "How can I ever repay you?" She asks them. Freeze says, "Now that you mentioned it, you could fix us a batch of those famous fudge brownies you make for PTA nights." JJ nods his head in agreement while he rubs his belly and licks his lips. "You got it boys." Miss Swisher tells them. "I will have you a batch ready tomorrow." She tells them. The two boys give Miss Swisher a hug then they leave.

Now the next day was Wednesday. The day before senior graduation. Miss Taylor calls JJ into her class as he was leaving to go home. "I have your grade." She tells JJ. "You do?" JJ asks. "Is it passing?" JJ asks. "Remember I deducted from your grade during the concert, right?" She tells JJ, "Yeah I know." JJ says. "I just want to know if it's passing?" She shows JJ his grade. "It reads A+. "Wow, Miss Taylor." JJ says. "An A+," He asks her. "Yes, JJ." She tells him. "An A+."

"Wow, really?" JJ says. "That's awesome." JJ tells her. "What you did for Mr. Swisher was nothing short of a miracle," Miss Taylor tells JJ. "You deserved an A+." He gives her a hug and turns to leave the classroom.

He turns back to her and says, "You're wrong, Miss Taylor." He tells her. "Why do you say that JJ?" She asks him. "Because it's not what I did for Swish," he tells her. "It was what Swish did for me." Miss Taylor smiles and says, "You did a lot of growing up this year, didn't you?" JJ nods his head and turns to leave the room.

CHAPTER 16

ODE TO SWISH

That brings us to this moment.

Here he was at the podium of his graduation, June 12th, 1996. One day before his 18th birthday. Reflecting upon what had really happened this year. Preparing to give the valedictorian speech for his class. Not for himself, but for someone else. Lord knows he wasn't an academic genius. Someone more deserving than himself. A special person that had changed the way he looked at life. He was giving the speech in his stead, surely an honor. As he stood there waiting to speak, he reflected on how they have come to this moment. It seemed so long ago.

"Good morning, my fellow students and faculty and administrators and parents and honored guests." "My name is Jonathan Jenkins." "Here I am giving the valedictorian speech." "This speech is much more deserving to someone else." "His name was Benjamin Swisher."

"I met Benjamin Swisher close to the first day of school." "At the time I thought how odd he was." "I thought how weird a person." "But now I realize that Benjamin was the epitome of the slogan, "You can't judge a book by its' cover." "Benjamin was the most talented, the smartest, the most gifted, but more important the most loving, most caring person you could ever want to meet." "You know we stand here and judge each other on how great we look and nice clothes we have." "And the fancy cars we drive and how much money we have and how much jewelry we have." "Not Benjamin, he didn't want or care about any of those material earthly things." "Benjamin just wanted to be your friend."

"Now that I look at it." "I look at all of us." "And I realize we are the weird ones." "We are the odd ones." "Now that I look at it." "Benjamin was the only normal person on earth." "I believe God put Benjamin on this earth as a role model to us to show us how we're supposed to treat each other." "To show us the important things on earth." "Love, respect, kindness." "Benjamin was that all wrapped in one package."

"Do you know the Bible says in Hebrews 13:2 KJV" "Be not forgetful to entertain strangers; for thereby some have entertained angels unawares."

"Swish was an angel put on earth on loan to us by God to come show us how we should be living." "We didn't realize what a gift we had until God took him back." "I'm going to miss the little fella." "Tagging around with me." "My little shadow." "Blowing up my game." "Because the girls thought he was cuter than me."

"Benji, if you can hear me." "Your best friend is going to miss ya." JJ says as he kisses his two fingers and points up to the sky. Then he goes and touches the seat that's reserved for the valedictorian and goes to his seat. As he goes to have a seat Freeze stands up and starts yelling "Swish!" "Swish!" "Swish!" Then the whole crowd begins to chant "Swish!" "Swish!" "Swish!"

A week after graduation they had Swish's funeral. Eight guys from the school, 4 from the basketball team and 4 from the football team, including JJ and Freeze, were pallbearers. After the funeral Freeze and JJ went and sat in the park. The two sat there reminiscing about the school year.

"Man, that was some send off for Benji wasn't it?" JJ says. "Yeah, I know." Freeze says, "He was something else." They sit there in silence for a minute. Then JJ says, "Man did you see Kayla dressed in a widow's garb?" "Hat with black veil included," JJ says. "Yeah man." Freeze says. "I saw her." "Did Swish turn her out or what?" They give each other a high five.

Then JJ says, "It was about 1000 people there." "Even the mayor of the city." JJ says. "Man, Swish went out like a boss." Freeze says. "That's for sure." JJ says. "When I go out that's how I wanna go out." Freeze says. A moment of silence. Then Freeze says, "I sure was mean to him." "What do you mean?" JJ says. "There you go, being down on yourself." JJ warns him. "Trekking down Misery Road." "I was though." Freeze says. "I hung him on the flagpole." "And busted water balloons on him."

"You know what?" JJ says. "Mr. Sad Sack." "I'm not gonna let you dog yourself like that." "Because of you Swish was on the basketball team and football team." "Man, how you stood up to Mr. Smith that day." "Man, I would rather stand up to a pride of lions than stand up to Mr. Smith." "And because of you Swish went to the senior prom, with a date and didn't die a virgin." They give each other a high five on that. "Because of you he had a decent funeral." "Man, what are you talking about?" "You made the last days of his life the best days of his life." JJ tells him.

Freeze thinks about it. "Yeah, I did," Freeze says after he has thought about it. Freeze says, "Yeah but I got to admit something, though." "Little man made me grow up into a real man." Freeze says,

"You got that right." JJ says. "He did the same for me." They both sit there in silence. "Yeah, I'm gonna miss him still." JJ says. "I don't think I'm gonna smile for a long time." He says with a big sigh. "Oh really?" Freeze says. "Well, I'm gonna fix that for you." Freeze says reaching into his backpack. "You are?" JJ says. "What magic potion you got you going to fix it?" JJ asks. "Watch this." Freeze says. "The magic potion is called H20." He gets a bottle of water out of his bag. Then he dumps the bottle of water on top of JJ's head. Freeze grabs his bag and takes off running.

JJ is huffing catching his breath from the water going over his face. "Oh, it's on now." JJ says as he grabs a bottle of water out of his bag and grabs his bag and goes running after Freeze.

Epilogue

KAYLA'S SURPRISE

Four years later March 2000. Freeze and JJ are at JJ's house playing video games. They are home for Spring break. Freeze is going to Michigan playing football and JJ is going to USC playing basketball. The two are on the computer playing video games.

"We're back to school in two days." Freeze says. "Yes, me to USC and you to Michigan." JJ says. One more semester to go," Freeze says. "Then we will be graduates," Freeze says. "Yeah, we gonna whoop y'all ass when y'all come play us next week." JJ says, "Yeah just be glad that I'm playing football and you playing basketball. I would have your number." Freeze says. "Yeah, talk is cheap." JJ says. The phone rings. "I gotta answer that." JJ says. "It might be moms."

"Yeah, don't let that be the reason that you get whooped in this game." Freeze says. JJ answers the phone. He comes back and tells Freeze. "That was Kayla on the phone." "Oh yeah," Freeze says. "What did she want?" "I haven't seen her in quite some time." "I don't know." JJ says. "She said she had something important to show us and needed us to come over right away." JJ says. "Okay," Freeze says. "Did she leave her address?" "Yeah, here it is right here." "1137 Fairmont Drive," JJ says. "Okay we can walk over there." "That's just down the street," Freeze says."

The two head for the address written down on the paper. "I wonder what she wants?" JJ says as they are walking to her house. "I don't know?" Freeze says. "But we gonna find out." Freeze says. Freeze and JJ come up to the address Kayla has given them. Freeze rings the doorbell. Kayla answers the door in what looks like pj's.

"Hey." Kayla says. "How my homies doing?" She says. They embrace and walk in the apartment. "Forgive my appearance." Kayla says. "But I have someone I want you to meet." "Hold on," Kayla says. She goes back to the bedroom and brings out a bright skin little boy with red hair. Looks to be about three to four years old.

"Oh, Kayla you are babysitting, huh?" Freeze says as she is holding the little boy's hand. "Not exactly." Kayla says. "What do you mean not exactly?" JJ asks. "Well fellas." Kayla says, "This is Benjamin Thomas Swisher Jr." They both look down at the little boy wide eyed. The little boy says, "Would you be my friend?"

Freeze just stands there gawking while JJ passes out. "JJ you okay?" Kayla says "JJ." "Freeze don't just stand there." "See about your friend." Kayla says to Freeze. Freeze and Kayla stoop down and try to revive JJ.